"I heard you're si... the receiver.

"Yep," I answered curtly.

"You see a doctor?"

"Yep."

"Is it serious?"

"Nope."

"Ginny? Why did you spill milk on my head?"

I hung up.

Hal called back. "I'd like to know what made you so angry," he said impatiently. "I thought we were having a great time together."

"We were."

"What happened?"

"Nothing."

"You don't dump milk on someone for nothing. Do you realize that now everybody in school thinks that you and I had some tremendous secret going on?"

"Well, we did."

"What secret? We were dating, that's all."

The silence between us on the phone got bigger and bigger.

Bantam Sweet Dreams Romances
Ask your bookseller for the books you have missed

Secrets

Anna Aaron

BANTAM BOOKS
TORONTO · NEW YORK · LONDON · SYDNEY

RL 6, IL age 11 and up

SECRETS
A Bantam Book / June 1983

Cover photo by Pat Hill

ISBN 0-553-23510-9

Published simultaneously in the United States and Canada

*Bantam Books are published by Bantam Books, Inc. Its trademark,
consisting of the words ''Bantam Books'' and the portrayal of a
rooster, is Registered in U.S. Patent and Trademark Office and in
other countries. Marca Registrada. Bantam Books, Inc., 666 Fifth
Avenue, New York, New York 10103.*

PRINTED IN THE UNITED STATES OF AMERICA

O   0 9 8 7 6 5 4 3 2 1

Secrets

Chapter One

I completely forgot my toothache when I saw the boy in faded denim overalls launch himself out of the back of the pickup truck.

I was sitting on Mrs. Harley's front lawn. The brakes squealed as the truck came to a stop in the driveway. The boy swung his legs up from the open truck bed in an easy graceful motion, and for a moment he seemed to be suspended between the sky and the earth. Honey-colored hair, long but not too long, whipped away from a wide, clear forehead. He looked about seventeen, maybe sixteen. Not tall but not short either. Generous mouth, nice curved eyebrows. I couldn't quite make out the color of his eyes.

The boy swerved his wide shoulders around; any instant he would see me sitting cross-legged and barefoot on the lawn in my yellow shorts and unicorn T-shirt next to Mrs. Harley's two-year-old son Jason, who was digging his front teeth into the tip of a thick black crayon.

Normally I would have whipped the crayon out of Jason's hand, because I took my responsibilities as a baby-sitter very seriously, but instead I waited for the boy's eyes to meet mine. Would he smile? Wave? Wink? Would he just go about his business, or would he swagger over and introduce himself?

Frankly, my attitude toward boys wasn't the greatest. The boys I met didn't have any idea about how to make a girl feel special. Their idea of romance was to grab you and try to make mashed potatoes of your mouth; and most of them seemed all wrapped up in their baseball gloves or the way they dribbled a basketball, except when they ogled you and said brainless things like, "Hey, Ginny, you wanna get married to me for a couple of weeks?"

That's why it probably didn't bother me at all when the boy in the faded denims looked right through me as if I were made of glass. I hated him, but only for about half a second.

Naturally you resent it when some boy who doesn't even notice you can trigger a whole series of chemical reactions in you: ice and steam, scared and happy, as if all the neurons and ganglions in your body had minds of their own, especially the five million new cells my bio teacher said get born every *minute.*

Then the boy spun around to unlatch the back end of his truck, and the hammer hanging from the loop of his overalls whirled out from his waist.

I guess I was a bit of a jerk because I couldn't stop hoping that maybe the boy really did have a good reaction to me like I had to him and was only hiding it because girls were sometimes sarcastic when they knew a boy liked them. I suddenly wanted to run over and grab his arm and tell him, "But I don't have a sarcastic bone in my body!"

And I imagined him blushing handsomely with embarrassment and saying, "Could I have your phone number?"

But of course we didn't say either of those things, he and I, and I was positive he didn't have the slightest interest in me. I snatched the black crayon away from little Jason, who was beginning to make soup out of it.

Meanwhile, the boy started taking big bags of cement from the back of the truck. Then he unloaded a wheelbarrow with the help of the driver of the truck, a thin man of about fifty with a black mustache. But I didn't see much of the unloading because a fist flew right into my eye.

The fist belonged to Jason. "I want my crayon!" he said and yowled.

Immediately I caught Jason's wrists and hauled him toward the house. He kicked me a few times, halfheartedly. I had visions of my punched eye blossoming into a swollen black-and-blue lump and the boy in the faded overalls wincing when he saw me.

Sneaking a quick look back before I shut Jason and myself into the house, I noticed the boy stripping off his shirt; lots of muscles were showing. All those lumps that boys seem to admire on their bodies usually strikes me as awfully vain and macho, pure ugh, but on him the muscles were different.

I locked the door behind us. Jason tried to bite me but missed. Then he settled down with his toy dump truck as if nothing had happened, largely because I gave him a ginger ale. He was a two-year-old ginger ale junkie. He could get the sodas out of the fridge, but he couldn't get them open. I was sort of his ginger ale connection. I usually used it to blackmail him into good behavior. I hated being a ginger ale pusher, but when you're a baby-sitter and you're desperate, you'll do almost anything.

Mrs. Harley had hired me to baby-sit for a week or so until her mother arrived to take over. Mrs. Harley was going back to school in order to go back to work in order to help pay for the construction of a new addition to her house where her mother could live. I felt angry that Mrs. Harley hadn't taught her son not to punch people in the eye.

A mirror in the living room reflected the first stages of a swollen eye. As I was inspecting it, I heard a man's voice yell something I couldn't understand. Moving closer to the window, I heard the boy answer, "Uncle Jeff, believe me, I can handle it!"

"Don't carry such big loads! You'll wreck yourself, and your mother'll blame *me*."

"OK, Uncle Jeff. I *reckon* I won't make a *wreck* of myself."

The boy's voice. The boy's voice was loud, but not coarse or harsh. It wasn't deep, but it wasn't high-pitched, either. It was a nice voice, nicer than nice.

Jason was stabbing crayons at his dump truck, and I was still thinking about the boy's voice when the telephone rang.

"Ginny, you're going to hate me. Totally hate me."

"Why, Pam?"

"I can't come over today. Bert phoned and asked me to go with him, help him shop around for a suitcase for his trip to Colorado to visit his aunt and uncle."

A bag of cement appeared, bouncing past Mrs. Harley's window on the shoulder of the boy with honey-colored hair.

"Do you hate me?"

"My left thumb will never forgive you, Pam."

I shifted my gaze from the window to Jason.

"I have this fear," Pam said, sniffling, "that Bert is going to get off the plane in Colorado, tear my number out of his book, light a match, burn it, and scatter the ashes."

"Pam, stop worrying! Bert is crazy about you."

"Every once in a while I catch him staring at my nose. Ginny, I swear Bert thinks my nose is weird."

"He's only going away for three or four weeks, Pam."

"Your way is the best, Ginny, you don't get hung up on one guy. Hey, remember that Marx Brothers poster of mine you liked? I passed a store that had it, and I bought one for you. Can I come over when you're baby-sitting tomorrow and bring it to you?"

After Pam and I hung up, I listened for the voice of the boy outside. Jason was calmly pouring ginger ale into his dump truck. Did I want Pam to come the next day? She might spoil my meeting the boy. Not that I thought she was prettier, just totally different. I was jealous of her plump curves; she was jealous of my slender curves. I should have told her not to come. Why didn't I? Probably I couldn't say no to Pam because I hated feeling guilty.

You could say I sort of had a sweet tooth for analyzing myself.

Maybe one of the reasons I analyzed things too much had to do with my sister Laura. Laura is so beautiful. I was baby-sitting to save money for a gift for Laura and her fiancé, Alan, who were getting married in September. Alan and Laura are definitely Beautiful People. As a matter of fact, my mom and dad are also BPs. I'm definitely no ugly duckling, but I *am* the Ordinary Person of the family, even though *they* are always telling me how special and pretty I am.

Well, anyway, analyzing wouldn't help me

meet the boy who was shouldering sacks of cement outside.

When Mrs. Harley came home, a yard of textbooks in her arms, I was washing ginger ale out of Jason's dump truck. She asked Jason if he'd had a good time. He smiled like an angel. She asked me how Jason had been. I smiled like an angel. She stared dubiously at my rainbow eye.

I found myself hoping—when I put my hand on the doorknob to go—that the boy wouldn't be there to see my poor swollen eye. Also another voice inside me was hoping that he *would* be there. I imagined myself opening the door and his saying with that grin, "Hey, that's a grand and glorious eye!"

Of course, my answer would be relaxed yet sophisticated. "I'll bet you tell that to all the girls with black eyes."

Or maybe the first thing he would say to me would take a tough guy Humphrey Bogart tone: "Go home and slap a steak on that eye, baby! Take a cab, my treat."

To which I would answer, equally streetwise, "Thanks, but no thanks, Bogie. I pay my own way."

"You got spunk, kid. I like spunk in a dame. I'll send my chauffeur to pick you up for dinner."

"Forget it, Bogie. You don't care about the real me. You just want to chalk up another conquest. . . ."

Still imagining flashy conversations with the boy, I opened the front door and stepped outside. The truck was there. The black mustache on the boy's uncle was there. The boy wasn't there, which caused a wave of relief but also one of disappointment.

Walking swiftly away from the house and down the street in the direction I lived, I pretended to be scratching my eyebrow so no one on the street would see my rainbow eye. Behind me I heard the boy's uncle shout, "Hal! Bring me the blueprint, will you, please?"

Hal. Now the boy had a name. I still didn't know what color his eyes were. Would he be there again tomorrow?

Hal. He could be a million different kinds of boys. I told myself it was dangerous feeling the way I did.

Hal. Hal and Ginny.

All the way home I kept scratching my eyebrow.

Chapter Two

That night I dreamed about Hal and my friend Pam—something about her nose—but when I woke up, the pieces of the dream blew away from me.

The summer air flowing in the window carried with it a memory of the sunlight in the tangles of his hair. My imagination brought him knocking on the door of my room with a breakfast tray for me: toast, coffee, juice, poached egg, one long-stemmed rose in a slender glass vase.

"What makes you look so beautiful when you wake up?" he would probably say.

"Thinking about you," I would answer in a husky voice.

Thinking about Hal and me, I got up and made my way to the mirror. My black eye, not as black as I feared, just needed makeup. What was that wonderful, scary sensation bopping all around under my rib cage? Hello, Hal, my name is—

I squeezed into my one-piece black bathing suit, the one with gaps cut out in some daring places. I could see myself splashing with Jason in the swimming tank in Mrs. Harley's backyard. Boys usually responded.

How would I look to Hal? Would he like flowing chestnut hair, dry sometimes, but bouncy—not quite my mother's gorgeous hair, of course. Would he like warm gray eyes, excellent lashes and brows, mouth only a fraction too wide, skin blemish-free (well, almost), neck a wee bit too long, bust acceptable, hips a trifle narrow compared to my sister Laura's, which were *perfect*, legs good, very, very good, but not so good as Laura's?

At breakfast Mom said, "Don't forget your dentist appointment after you leave Mrs. Harley's."

I kissed her as I started out the door. What would Hal think if he knew I was terrified of a dentist's drill grinding deep in my molars?

I arrived only a few minutes late with my black bathing suit concealed beneath a loose powder-blue terry cloth top and a flared white tennis skirt.

There was no truck there. And no Hal.

Mrs. Harley did a few last-minute zigzags to find her car keys and eyeglasses, then dashed to her station wagon while I kept hoping to see a gorgeous and magical construction truck.

"Ginny! Ginny!" Jason's voice snapped me out of my daydreams. He was waving around a slab of silly putty that he had been stretching and shaping into a figure. "Watch the man die!" His fist hovered over the blob, and he smashed it flat.

Boys are so violent. Was Hal?

I told Jason I'd play hide 'n' seek with him, but my feet kept drifting over to the kitchen window for a glance at the driveway. Go ahead, Ginny, let a complete stranger make you act like an idiot.

I tried to visualize his face; it wouldn't come clear—only the workman's boots, wide shoulders, the hard, curved muscles, and, yes, the honey-colored hair.

A squeal of brakes in the driveway made me jump. The truck. The uncle with the black mustache was at the wheel. A moon-faced, bald workman got out of the other side. Black letters on the side of the truck: Jackson Construction Company. But no one swung his legs up from the open truck bed, no workman's boots landed on the asphalt driveway with the powerful grace of an athlete.

My hopes and excitement shriveled like a huge balloon deflating to a little piece of wrinkled rubber. He'd probably only been helping his uncle out for the day. All the scenes I had concocted in my mind—Hal and I leaping on the sand dunes, driving for hours up in farm country, dancing, the feel of his cheek, his hands—were all wasted.

"Ginny, what are you doing!" a small voice said, whining. "I hid myself so you'd never find me. You said we were playing hide 'n' seek, but you aren't!"

The next hour wasn't exactly my idea of heaven on earth. Even my ginger ale strategy was a bust; I gave Jason his usual ginger ale fix, but the moment he finished sucking up the soda, he went hyper on me again.

Baby-sitting for Jason Harley, or any other two year old, can really wear you out, especially when you're kicking yourself for having failed to think of anything to say to the first boy you ever encountered who really made your heart fly and who probably had disappeared out of your life forever.

I could imagine my sister Laura comforting me. "Ginny, when you meet Mr. Right, he'll know he's got a treasure!"

Laura was always conspiring with my folks to build up my ego. I should have been grateful; other kids had sisters and parents who always put them down, like Pam's, her father particularly.

Anyway, thinking of Laura didn't help because Laura would soon be married to Alan, and her room down the hall from me would be empty. I felt as if I had a million empty rooms inside me. I wanted to cry, but the tears wouldn't come.

And then, right outside the window, a voice called out, "Hey, Uncle Jeff! Sorry I'm late!"

Chapter Three

Of course, I had to resist popping my head out the window to stare at Hal as he jogged past the truck to join his uncle and the other workman, but I did catch a glimpse of his honey-colored hair rising and falling as he ran, the hammer jumping in the loop of his faded overalls, his mouth curving on the verge of a smile.

But something had changed. I heard it in the sound of his voice. Staying close to the half-open window, I heard him say, "Sorry I'm late. I got all the chores done, then Mom called long distance."

"She OK?" his uncle asked gruffly.

"Said she loves it." Tightness, that was the difference in Hal's voice, tightness in the way he said "she loves it."

Call it intuition, or whatever, but I knew something serious was troubling him. Maybe I could help. Sure, I said to myself, you don't even know the boy, and already you're building him into some kind of romantic figure who desperately needs you.

Well, pretty soon I got Jason settled in front of the television for his favorite show, "Sesame Street," a repeat, and he went giggling away into videoland with Big Bird and Cookie Monster.

After Cookie Monster came a half hour of Popeye. Jason turned the volume up. I turned it down. His mouth made like an air-raid siren; his face grew beet red. The air-raid siren won; I turned up the volume.

The doorbell was a welcome relief from the sounds of Popeye digesting his spinach and whacking his archenemy's hundred-watt nose. I flung open the door, ready to yell, "Hi, Pam! Boy, am I glad to—"

The face in the doorway was definitely not Pam's.

"Hi, I'm one of the workmen. Can I please use your phone?"

It was him. He. Hal. My tongue felt paralyzed. My brain got suddenly disconnected.

Numb, I pointed toward the kitchen.

"Thanks," Hal said and smiled, his eyes

crinkling. "Sure would be a lonely world without telephones."

I nodded. He went into the kitchen. My stomach descended at supersonic speed toward the center of the earth.

"Excuse me," he said, grinning apologetically in the kitchen doorway, "but I can't find the phone."

"Oh, no, I'm sorry." I eked out the words in a humble, watery voice, and my face started the beginning of, I guess, a pretty foolish smile. "I forgot."

He chuckled. "You forgot you don't have a phone in your own kitchen?"

"I don't live here. I'm just baby-sitting."

Being within touching distance of Hal made me shaky, though my voice, amazingly, came out pretty mellow; I was gaining control over my nervousness, but it still seemed as if I were giving lessons in how to act like an idiot.

"No wonder you forgot where the phone is. Kids can drive you up the wall." His friendly tone made her feel much less stupid.

"Jason's nice, most of the time." I realized I was looking into his eyes, brown eyes, not ordinary brown, more like hazel, hazel eyes, warm eyes that left me feeling soft, buttery.

"That's nice." Hal seemed to be waiting for

me to say something, but I didn't know what. All I wanted to do was to go on staring at him.

"About the phone," he said politely.

"The phone?"

He nodded with a curious expression that might have meant he was wondering if I was having fun at his expense. "Maybe the phone is in the bathroom," he said cheerfully, without a trace of sarcasm.

My tongue, which had momentarily turned to stone, came alive again. "It's there on the desk."

As he picked up the telephone, sunlight streamed through the window and onto his hair. His fingertips dialing the phone were blunt, powerful, one fingernail all purple, as if he had hit it with a hammer; and he wore the most curious silver ring with little inlaid gems that spelled a word I couldn't make out.

"Hello, can I talk to Rita Stone, please? She's taking the life class in drawing."

I escaped into the kitchen. I didn't want to hear him speak to another girl.

"Hi, Rita! How's your hot little paintbrush?"

I yanked open the fridge—deciding to make an early lunch—hauled out the peanut butter jar, and slammed the fridge door loudly. I grabbed the bread, banged a copper-bottomed pot down on the stove to make hot chocolate to go with the peanut butter sandwiches, and generally created as much noise as I could so I wouldn't have to overhear Hal's conversation with his hot little paintbrush girl.

Of course, I heard every word.

"He sounds like a terrific teacher. 'Course I didn't mind. I *enjoy* driving you! No, he knew I'd be late. Don't feel that way. Stick with me, kid, I'll make a man out of you yet. What's wrong with being a man?"

He laughed at something she said.

Envious of his girl, whoever she was, I stared down into the swirls of peanut butter at the bottom of the jar.

"I'll pick you up as soon as I finish work. Rita, you really enjoying it? Great! Hey, why does the dolphin cross the road? To get to the other tide! He crosses the road on porpoise. Get it? You're not laughing, Rita. If you don't laugh, it means you don't love me! Pick you up at six?"

By the time he hung up, the rest of my summer was ruined. Rita.

Then he popped into the kitchen, offered me a thank-you wave of his hand, and vanished, leaving behind, however, a few choice words that really bugged me. "Sure was nice finding the telephone with you!"

That last remark might have been kind of fun, if I hadn't just discovered that he already had a girlfriend named Rita, probably a stuck-up snooty type if she didn't even enjoy his joke about the dolphin crossing the road on porpoise, which wasn't all that funny but was sort of witty. And if you like a boy, at least you can try to laugh a little.

I never liked snooty girls, and I was sure I would never again like anybody named Rita.

Then I thought maybe he wasn't going steady with her, maybe he saw other girls also, and maybe what he said to me about finding the telephone together was meant as an offering of friendship.

Don't be a fool, Ginny, I warned myself.

Still, you never know what a boy might be feeling. Boys always want their own way. They never seem to care about girls as individuals. They talk as if girls are just objects. You never know when they are going to ball up their fists and punch each other. They're nasty. They're mean. And sometimes they are so heartbreakingly *cute*.

So there we were, me inside the house slapping peanut butter on slices of raisin bread, Hal outside lugging two-by-fours and hammering nails, and little Jason glued to the cartoon show following Popeye.

A phone call from Pam interrupted my thoughts about Hal.

"Ginny, I can't come over. Bert just called and he asked me, he'd like me, he really *wants* me to go to the airport with him, with them, his parents and brother."

"That's nice, Pam." I tried to keep the pleasure out of my voice, pleasure that I'd have Hal all to myself.

"Ginny, I'm so scared Bert will forget me. On top of that, my father blames Bert for my low grades last year, and he says I'm lazy and I'd better apply for a scholarship because he won't pay for college. Ginny, I'll never get a scholarship! Do you think I should tell Bert I love him?"

"I don't know, Pam."

"I'm sorry, all I do is blab about me. I really miss us being together, Ginn. We haven't seen each other all week. Let's go to the beach Saturday!"

I tried to believe she meant it. Sure, Pam still thought we were special friends, but how could I stay special friends when she hardly had time to see me between Bert and the part-time job she got because her father wouldn't buy her the clothes she liked. The trouble with girls is, guys gets in our blood, and suddenly there isn't time for anyone but them. Before Bert, Pam and I double-dated all the time; before Bert, we spent hours in her basement falling in and out of love with Billy Joel and Rick Springfield; before Bert, we ate mountains of popcorn at horror movies together . . . before Bert.

A tear plopped from my cheek onto my arm. Meanwhile, Batman and Robin were leaping into their Batmobile with Jason watching bug-eyed.

A hammer was clicking against something metal in the backyard. "Grab that, will you!" Hal's uncle shouted.

Maybe I should bring some iced tea out to Hal and the other two men. But shouldn't he make the first move? Grow up, Ginny, this is the twentieth century! Maybe I'm not the right person for the twentieth century.

My mind wandered to an old movie I had seen, *On the Beach*. Radioactivity from nuclear explosions was killing off the last surviving people on earth, in Australia. Would I wait for Hal to make the first move if he was Gregory Peck and I was Ava Gardner dying in Australia?

"Mind if I join you?" I imagined myself saying to him.

Hal would look up from his drink—he'd be wearing the uniform of an American submarine commander—and say, "I like a woman who speaks her mind."

He'd stand, hold a chair for me, his eyes brooding, mysterious, a crooked smile on his lips. I'd sit. His naval insignia would glint in the candlelight. "Have you ever been in love?" he'd ask.

"Never," I would say, trembling.

"Neither have I," he would say. "We haven't much time."

Hal—the movie version of him—was reaching out to put his hand over mine when suddenly the film snapped. A loud knocking at the back door got me to my feet unwillingly.

The person at the door was Hal, the real-life Hal, looking a little sheepish around the edges.

"The phone is definitely not in the kitchen," I said pertly, casting a brilliant smile at him.

"Sorry I smarted off at you," he said, spacing the words carefully.

I tried aiming my eyes so they were on a collision course with his eyes. "You were only being funny," I said.

"Well, it was dumb."

"Not really."

There were flecks of other colors in the

warm hazel of his eyes, tiny, tiny touches of bronze and copper.

"Anyway, I'm sorry," he added.

"You don't have to be. It was nothing."

"I'm glad it didn't bother you."

"It didn't at all."

Our eyes, as we talked, kept drifting away and meeting and breaking off. A smell of sawdust wafted off his hair. A whine of electric saws drowned our voices, then stopped. From the backyard, a gruff voice shouted, "Hal, get that thing out and get it cleaned up!"

"OK, Uncle Jeff!" Hal called back. He twisted the underside of his elbow to show me a smear of blood and a thick wood splinter stuck under the skin.

"You have a sewing needle or something so I can dig out the splinter?"

I found a needle. He washed his elbow with soap and water, the muscles in his arms moving smoothly.

"You better let me do it," I said.

"Thanks."

The needle, when I sterilized the tip in a match flame, glowed red hot. I pressed my fingers on the skin around the splinter and probed delicately with the needle. But the only way to get it out was to dig. When the needle went in deep, Hal's body stiffened, and he grunted.

Drops of sweat beaded my forehead as I jabbed the needle at the fragment of wood.

Hal smiled grimly, as if we were having a tea party he couldn't wait to leave.

Digging around in somebody's skin was not my idea of a great way to start a relationship.

"There!" I had it out, caught on the blackened tip of the needle.

His face relaxed into gratitude. "You have a great future in the splinter business."

I felt suddenly weak in the knees, and all I could say was, "How about a little hydrogen peroxide?"

"Sure!" The way he licked his lips made me chuckle. "I'll have mine with milk and sugar."

I poured peroxide and watched it foam over the broken skin. Then a Band-Aid. Why didn't he introduce himself? Why didn't I?

"Well," he said, grinning and flicking his right hand up to his forehead in a smart salute, "don't fire until you see the whites of their eyes!"

My face must have looked absolutely baffled.

"That means thanks a lot," he whispered.

The back door closed behind him. Oh, I wanted to give him such a kick in the pants! Hey, you didn't even ask my name! Someone pulls your skin apart with a sewing needle, the least you can do is introduce yourself!

On the other hand, I couldn't stay angry at him because I had a whole bunch of new little details that fascinated me. Like why did the first two knuckles on both his hands look so rough and swollen? Like what was the word in some foreign alphabet in little green stones on his ring? I had a million questions! What's your favorite food? You have any pets? How was your childhood? Are you in love with Rita?

So, instead, I unscrewed Jason from the television set, finally fed him a peanut butter sandwich and then swept the two of us outside, where we splashed around in the circular above-ground pool behind the house.

Of course, the water made the black material of my bathing suit very slick. I kept sneaking a glance across the lawn toward Hal, his uncle, the workman, their electric saw screaming, their hammers pounding wood frames.

But not once did I catch Hal looking at me. I felt about as sexy as a kerosene lamp.

Chapter Four

I woke up with a headache. I wanted to blame somebody, but who? For two days running, Hal had not come to work at Mrs. Harley's house.

"Ginny, what time will they be here?" Mom called.

"Nine-thirty!"

Electricity crackled in my chestnut hair as I brushed it. My blue bikini looked OK.

Downstairs in the kitchen, a few minutes later, swiss cheese, lettuce, mustard, and mayonnaise went flying in between slabs of whole wheat bread. Mom and I worked like an assembly line; she believed in making three times as much food as you needed, in case other kids forgot their sandwiches.

Night or day Mom never had a hair out of

place. She looked an easy ten years younger than she was.

"What's happening, Ginn?" She had a special tone of voice she used when she sensed I wasn't on top of the world.

"I'm fine, Mom."

"Are you really?"

She knew me like a book, only sometimes I tore out the pages I didn't want anyone to read.

"I'm having a nice summer, Mom."

"Nice?" She pushed a strand of hair away from my eyes.

How can you tell your mother that a boy you hardly know makes your insides feel like melted butter?

"You seem so preoccupied, Ginny."

"Well, things aren't going so great with me and Pam."

"Friendships ought to make you happy, not bothered."

"You always told me you have to work at a friendship."

"If you're sure it's worth it."

We were stuffing the foil-wrapped sandwiches into a beach bag along with plastic bottles of suntan lotion.

"There must be other girls besides Pam."

"We had so much fun last year. I just keep hoping she'll get back to being herself."

Mom laughed, I couldn't figure why. "Just remember, Ginny, you are somebody important, you're beautiful, you're bright, you're the cream of the crop, and you deserve the best."

Why, lately, whenever Mom tried so hard to build me up, did it feel like such a downer?

A horn honked outside. I grabbed a beach towel.

"Don't forget your first aid meeting tonight!"

"Love you, Mom!"

I jumped in the front seat beside Pam. She squeezed my hand, and I realized how much I'd missed her. From the backseat a chorus of voices greeted me—Rose, Gail, and Veronica. Pam had worked long hours to buy her little two-door, and she drove like it was made of glass. I kept quiet, stirring up memories of Hal, while the other girls gabbed behind us.

"So, I said I don't kiss on the first date."

"I bet you would if it was Jeremy Franklin!"

"Jeremy Franklin is a nerd."

"You're crazy! He's gorgeous!"

"He's a turkey!"

"He's a hunk!"

"He's gross!"

"Ginny, what do you think of Jeremy Franklin?"

I shrugged. "How about he's a gorgeous nerd?"

Groans from behind me.

At the first stoplight, Pam shook her thick, curly hair, smiled broadly, and handed me a candy box, like it was sort of a peace offering. Inside the box were six maple sugar leaves. We wrinkled our noses at each other; she knew I was bananas about maple sugar.

"How'd it go at the airport with Bert?"

"Terrible, but OK."

Getting near the beach, patches of sand appeared along the road, as did wildflowers, blue ones. I liked wildflowers because they seemed so unpredictable. I myself always seemed terribly predictable, though I didn't want to be. How do you stop being predictable?

Rose and Gail and Veronica were talking a mile a minute.

"Marty gave me such a dirty look when I told him my dad wants us home by eleven-thirty from now on. . . ."

"Don't you just hope the beach is *littered* with gorgeous boys? . . ."

"I saw the cutest beach jacket at Bambergers! . . ."

"You'd have died if you saw what Harriet Considine was wearing. . . ."

I wasn't much interested in talking. We hit the parking lot and jerked to a stop. In the distance there was a glitter of ocean. The other girls piled out and walked ahead, while Pam locked the car door.

"It's great having a friend you can tell all your secrets to," Pam said, easing her arm through mine.

And I thought of the secrets I never told anyone.

A park ranger on a black horse moved past the state park building and fast food concession toward the miles of sand dunes.

With our blankets and towels and bags, we headed toward a wide break between the dunes.

The black horse and ranger stopped near a girl sitting alone on a beach chair, a girl with long, copper-colored hair, who I figured was about a year older than I. The ranger and horse moved away toward the distant bird sanctuary, off limits to the public.

Ahead of us the girls chattered away.

"Look at the tall one with freckles!"

"I bet he's a snob."

"He looks like Roger Nugent."

"You need glasses!"

"Roger Nugent is a zero."

"I heard he's going out with Jill."

"Jill with Roger Nugent? She's got to be crazy!"

The girl with copper-colored hair, seated in the aluminum chair, had a white canvas on a small easel and a tripod in front of her. She had long slender legs stretched out on either side of the tripod. She touched the tip of a paintbrush to the surface of the canvas, and a blue dab appeared. My friends hardly noticed her. There were more interesting attractions where the waves tumbled and spilled.

We passed within yards of the girl, her tubes of paint, her jar of brushes. She was mixing blue on a palette smeared with other rich colors.

"There's a good spot near the lifeguard station!"

"Wait! How about farther down where the surfboards are?"

My eyes swung back toward the girl with copper hair. Her face was striking—heart-shaped with high cheekbones. She seemed completely absorbed in watching the sea gulls and the wild plums on a nearby sand dune. I envied her total concentration.

Above the tideline, we flapped out our blankets. Surfers, good-looking with sun-streaked hair tousled by the wind, ambled past with their multicolored boards.

Way back toward the sand dunes, the girl with copper-colored hair, her green bikini catching the sunlight, continued to paint.

Pam and I smeared gobs of white sunscreen over each other's shoulders and back. A couple of times she started compulsively to worry about Bert out loud and then stopped herself, making an effort, which I appreciated, to revive the fun the two of us had before Bert. But I wondered how long it would last when he came back. And would I be any different if I started spending time with a boy like Hal?

I stretched out on my stomach, closed my eyes, and let the sun sink deep into my skin. Pam lay her head in the small of my back and chatted away with the girls.

"We should've set our blanket near the lifeguard station."

"Those surfers were cute."

"One of them winked."

I'd heard this banter a thousand times before. Sea gulls overhead barked like puppies. My mind drifted lazily. An image appeared behind my closed eyes, the girl with copper hair, the bright liquid color on the paintbrush touching the naked white canvas.

I must have dozed. Beads of perspiration flowed along the edge of my suit. Music pulsed from beautiful Veronica's favorite rock station. I opened my eyes and looked out at the Atlantic Ocean. In the distance the waves crashed high and rough. A lone surfer way out, just a speck, was riding the back of a huge hump of water, very fast. He had picked a spot where the force of the sea was tremendous and dangerous, where one surfer had drowned the year before.

And he did something I had never seen anyone dare. As the huge wave swept him forward, he flung his feet upward and his hands down into a handstand on the tip of the surfboard.

A split second later he wiped out.

And when he recovered his board and strode out of the water and up the beach, I recognized him.

I knew he would head for the girl with copper hair. What was it he had said on the phone in Mrs. Harley's house?

"Hi, Rita! How's your hot little paintbrush?"

He went past our blankets, but he couldn't see my face. I didn't want him to.

He stood his board erect in the sand near her easel. He dried his honey-colored hair with a towel. Then he picked her up in his arms and carried her all the way down the beach to the water's edge.

I couldn't keep my eyes off them. They seemed like sweethearts, and yet you would have expected them to be laughing, but they looked, if not serious, not playful either.

He stood with her in his arms at the water's edge, waiting, staring toward the horizon, until the bigger waves had pulled back and there was a lull. Then he carried her into the water, chest deep. At that moment she just swam away from him. He watched her as she swam. She did an odd breaststroke, away from him and circling back. Then he picked her up again and carried her out of the breaking surf.

This time, as they headed toward us, I just didn't want to be there.

"I'm going for a soda," I blurted out, jumping up between Pam and Veronica.

"We've *got* soda."

"*And* a hamburger," I added decisively.

"What about your sandwiches?"

I grabbed some money from my bag and headed up the beach. Did he recognize me? Not likely with his arms full of his copper-haired Rita.

A few minutes later, I was relieved to be standing in a long line at the fast foods concession. For once in my life I was pleased to be in a slow line. The slower the better.

"Excuse me, I've got a splinter in my telephone."

Even before I turned around, I knew it was Hal right behind me.

"Hi," I said. My voice sounded awfully squeaky.

"Small world." His tanned skin set off the white of his teeth in a relaxed grin that clearly said, "I'm glad to see you!" I couldn't believe it was just by accident he happened to get in line right behind me, but how else?

"How's the food here?"

"I guess it's fast.

"Doing any first aid lately?" He flashed a smile that cut right into my ribs.

"Matter of fact, I'm on the local first aid squad."

"Like if somebody gets a broken heart, you put the stitches in?"

"I wouldn't know. I never had a broken heart."

"I hope you never do," he said softly, rubbing his chin. There was a flash of sadness in his eyes, as if he had suddenly traveled deep into himself and gotten lost for a moment; and just as suddenly he smacked the palms of his hands together and returned, a little too chipper, from wherever he had been.

"What lies on the bottom of the sea," he asked, "and just twitches and twitches?"

"I give up."

"A nervous wreck." He tried to keep a straight face but couldn't help laughing at his own joke.

And his eyes held fast to mine for just a brief moment. Was he trying to say he liked me? I couldn't tell. He had a way of making my chemistry go haywire. Especially that sudden, brief, inward look of his, like a door flung open for a fraction of a second on a cool, dark place, a place of secrets.

The line snaked toward the food counter where hot orange lights gleamed on the slowly rotating frankfurters.

"I saw you surfing. It looked dangerous."

"Actually I was scared out of my skull. You surf?"

I shook my head.

"You ought to try it."

Was he offering to show me?

A sharp voice cut between us. "Hey, what's your order, miss? These hot dogs are gonna get senile waitin' for you!"

Moments later we were separated, me paying the cashier for my cheeseburger and malt,

Hal still at the counter collecting a double order of french fries.

We had talked, and neither one of us had said our names. I was furious with myself.

I lingered over the ketchup as long as I could, but his order was taking a long time. I left.

Kicking my feet through the sand, I passed the girl with the copper hair. A sky, clouds, sand dunes, and the sea were taking shape on her canvas.

He could easily have asked me for my phone number, and yet if he had asked, I might have thought it was pretty rotten of him when he was so involved with another girl.

And maybe I just wasn't his type.

The rest of the afternoon went by in a blur. Without Hal. The girls set up our volleyball net, and some surfers joined us. I slapped the ball hard, shouted, laughed, flirted, but it was all a pretense. Even when we threw ourselves into the waves to cool off, nothing could disconnect my mind from the two distant figures on the blanket near the dunes.

The way he had carried her, as if she were fragile, down to the water and back, quite a distance, almost as if it was some kind of ceremony or something, suggested they had known each other a long time.

Frankly, it was a relief when Pam got sick, because it stopped me thinking about Hal.

It happened when the score was tied. Pam dropped the volleyball and clutched her leg in pain. Her skin was pale, clammy, sweating; she felt dizzy, nauseated. I recognized the symptoms from my first aid training: heat cramps and possible heat exhaustion.

We carried her to the first aid station. They gave her sips of cool salt water, put cool wet cloths on her forehead, and put her in front of a fan. Pam's mom drove out to get her, and I insisted on staying with her all the way home.

Veronica said she didn't mind driving Rose and Gail home in Pam's car, so we left them with a bunch of surfer types and the volleyball and the sand and waves and big blue sky and sea gulls and the two attractive people on the blanket near the dunes.

At noon the next day Pam called me to say thanks and to gossip. "Remember the boy who carried his girlfriend into the water and back?"

"You mean the girl who was painting?"

"Right! When Veronica brought my car back, she mentioned how he happened to get into our volleyball game after I got sick, and his name is Hal, and Veronica thinks he's terrific."

"Oh," I said.

"*And* it turns out the girl who paints isn't his girlfriend, she's his sister Rita. She can't walk, her legs are paralyzed."

"Oh," I said.

It was probably the smallest *oh* I ever said in my entire life.

Chapter Five

The day after Hal and I chatted in the fast food line, Mrs. Harley called me to say her mother had arrived and she no longer needed me to baby-sit for Jason. That was the end of Hal and me—almost.

I told myself there were plenty of other fish in the sea, but the other fish didn't give me goose pimples.

Summer was almost over, and I wanted to be involved with Hal before school began.

Finally I had an idea. It came to me at first aid headquarters, when the instructor wound up the lesson by asking for volunteers to canvass various neighborhoods. I remembered the Jackson Construction Company, looked through the phone book, spotted the address of Jeffrey Jackson, Hal's uncle, and volunteered to canvass that area.

I had to do something to see him again, even if I made a fool of myself. I couldn't forget Hal.

And I couldn't forget his sister. The stunning copper-haired girl with beautiful legs—lifeless legs, according to Pam—had caused an odd, sharp sensation in me, a sadness mixed with envy for the way she seemed to focus her whole being on the glistening oil colors and the canvas. I couldn't forget the calm in her face as Hal had carried her across the sand.

I chose a bright, sunny day to make the rounds of Hal's neighborhood. One by one, I rang the doorbells of the houses on the street, saving Hal's house for last.

"I'm canvassing for the First Aid Squad," I said at each house. "Do you have anyone in your family who needs special care or medicines in an emergency? Anyone with heart trouble or diabetes?"

At last I came to a house with cedar shingles, the last one on a dead-end street. The truck marked Jackson Construction Company was not in the driveway. When it came time to ring the doorbell, I hesitated.

I would feel horrible if Hal realized that my canvassing their house was no coincidence. But I had an irresistible urge to make some kind of contact, if not with him, with the things and people around him.

It was Rita who opened the front door.

"Hello! Can I help you?"

Even seated in a wheelchair, she radiated energy.

"Hi! I'm with the local First Aid Squad."

"Come on in!" She had a low voice, vibrant, an accent like her brother's, definitely not East Coast. Her long copper hair shimmered against a denim smock.

"It won't take long."

"I'm in no rush."

Her hands, on the rims of her chair wheels, were freckled with paint stains. As she propelled herself along a narrow blue-carpeted hallway leading into the living room, I experienced a sudden sense of awkwardness. She had looked beautiful and independent on the beach, but here in the confines of the house, the wheelchair made her seem smaller, vulnerable.

"I've been trying to paint with acrylics. The colors make me feel like a kid, like bubblegum and merry-go-rounds."

43

There was a joy in her face that almost hurt to see. A joy almost too naked.

"Do you like colors?"

"Absolutely!"

"Care for a soda?"

"Sure."

"You're the first human being I've talked to since my brother and uncle left for work this morning," she called from the kitchen.

Wheeling smoothly back into the living room with two paper cups and a green quart bottle of ginger ale, she set them down on a coffee table in front of me.

"I'm Rita Stone."

"Ginny. Ginny Barnes."

We shook hands. Her hand was dry and strong.

"I know I've seen you somewhere," I said, not enjoying the pretense.

"We only moved in with my uncle three weeks ago."

"Were you at Miller's Point beach Saturday with a boy who surfed?"

"My brother Hal, that's right!"

"Believe it or not, I had the honor of stabbing your brother with a burned sewing needle."

When I told her how Hal and I had met, she was amused. "I hope I'm not keeping you from your first aid work. Do you have time? Honestly?"

Time? I had an unquenchable greed to soak up anything that was part of Hal's world.

"You're the last house on my list. I'm free as soon as I explain this stuff." I gave her a card with the First Aid Squad number and other emergency phone numbers. I showed her the plastic first aid kit to be kept in the refrigerator with medicine and instructions for helping any household member with special problems.

"Can I see what you're painting?"

Delighted, Rita led me through the kitchen to a screened-in back porch and a stretched canvas on a three-legged easel facing the garden. Nailed against a wooden beam was an enlarged photo of Hal, a little younger than I knew him, holding a surfboard on his head and gazing directly into the lens, his features softened in a sunny unguarded smile, as if the person holding the camera were the center of his universe.

"Hal hates sitting still too long, so I also use his photograph."

Rita's portrait of Hal, taking shape in slashes of color on the white canvas, was so different from the quiet, realistic painting of sea gulls

45

I had seen her doing on the beach that I gasped.

"I want to paint the part of him he won't let anybody know, not even me."

"You're asking a lot of yourself."

"That's what makes it exciting. You ever try painting?"

"I sketch a little, but mostly I like interior decorating."

Rita clapped her hands. "Maybe you could help me with Hal's room. He asked me to redo it. The problem is his cage."

"You keep him in a cage?"

We giggled. I was pleased I could make her laugh. Could I make *him* laugh, too?

Hal's room definitely needed a change. Wallpaper with faded blue grapes, drab tartan carpet, beige window curtains, small yellow chest of drawers, and an oxblood leather armchair that made the curtains look like petticoats in a men's locker room.

And, as Rita had said, a cage. A glass and wire cage, three feet by four feet, about two feet high.

In the cage lay a snake, motionless, uncoiled, at least three feet long, on top of layers of wood chips. My skin crawled.

"*This*, Ginny, is a boa constrictor."

What do you say to a boa constrictor when

the sight of his thick, scaly skin makes you ill?

"You like snakes, Ginny?"

"They haven't been part of my circle of close friends, but I like them as belts." I edged away from the cage.

"See what I mean, Ginny? How do you put zing in a room when a snake is the center of attraction?"

My eyes soaked up every detail of the room, like the pictures on Hal's desk of Rita and him holding hands, about to jump from a low cliff toward a mass of shining water, and Hal and Rita as preteens, their arms around a dark-eyed, serious woman and a red-haired, grinning man.

"Are they your parents?"

Rita's eyes clouded. She nodded. I had the sense not to pursue it.

"Suppose," I offered, "you move the cage into that corner, make sort of a little jungle of potted plants all around it."

Rita brightened. "Yes, and maybe indirect lighting on the floor!"

My eyes traveled over the hastily made bed, the scattered shoes and shirts and tape decks. Being in his room gave me a kind of secret intimacy with Hal.

On the other hand, my heart sank when I

saw, hanging in his closet, a long, rubber-handled knife in a rubber sheath, a black underwater wet suit with flippers, a mask, and a lethal spear gun. Then there were his posters: a skydiver falling spread-eagled; a man harnessed to a red kite a thousand feet high; bricks crumbling under the blow of a karate fighter's forehead; a shark swerving past a diver.

If anything scares me more than a cold, scaly boa constrictor, it is sharks, knives, heights, and drowning.

"I'd like to do his room in sea and sky colors."

"And you could paint a rainbow on the wall that gets the least light."

"A rainbow would be perfect!" Rita's eyes glowed with pleasure. "My brother should be home pretty soon. We can tell him your ideas."

I hesitated. Cold feet, Ginny? My big toes were about forty below zero. I had dared enough already.

"Rita, I have to get home."

She wheeled to the front door with me and wrinkled her nose ruefully. "Wish I could keep you here."

"I'd love to stay, believe me."

Her smile was dazzling. "Will you come again,

Ginny? It's hard to make friends around here. Talk about lonely!"

It seemed to me I'd never met anybody less lonely in my life, and I envied her honesty.

"Rita, we're having a beach party next Saturday night. Why don't you come?" I'd meant all along to invite her.

"My wheelchair hasn't been fitted with antigravity rockets yet, so my brother would have to take me. Is that OK?"

Did she have any inkling of how terribly I wanted Hal to be there?

Somewhere in the middle of the night I woke up. Luminous hands on the clock pointed to three-thirty. Moonlight like a layer of snow spread across my blanket. Tears began streaming down my cheeks. Why?

First Rita in her wheelchair, then Hal on his surfboard, passed through my mind, and Pam, struggling with Bert, with her dad, and, finally, Laura, Laura getting married—too many images!

I rose from bed, sat cross-legged on the wooden bench under the window, my fingertips tracing the seam where Dad had glued the bench back together in my kindergarten days.

Would Dad like Hal? Would Mom and Laura?

How do you explain to them things like crying and not knowing why, without getting them worried? Not to speak of a boy who makes you come unglued.

On the way downstairs to get a glass of hot milk, I saw a crack of light under Laura's door. I knocked.

"Come in."

Sitting up in bed, she motioned me closer. "How's the world treating you at three o'clock in the morning?" Her voice betrayed a strain.

"Your wedding is going to be one of the great weddings of all time," I said glumly.

Laura laughed a hollow laugh. "Four more weeks. Going to miss me?"

"Nah."

We both laughed; a little nervously, I thought. She patted the bed, and I sat there, admiring her wispy bangs, layer-cut hair surrounding a perfect oval face, romantic dark eyes; no wonder Alan was head over heels about her.

"I think I'm too young to get married," she said airily. "I should wait until I'm at least thirty."

Airily, but I sensed her anxiety.

"You love each other, don't you, Laura?"

She nodded. "It's natural, I suppose, to be scared when the wedding day gets closer and closer," she said unconvincingly.

"Have you told Alan?"

"He's handling some terribly important lawsuits." Carelessly Laura brushed lint from the arm of her black Chinese bed jacket and managed a smile.

"Why don't you talk to Mom?" I urged.

"Why don't *you*?" she countered.

"*Me*? I'm fine!"

"You've been moping around the last few days with boy trouble written all over your face."

I bristled at the way she copped out on her own problems by throwing the weight on me. "You're seeing things, Laura!"

"Tell me you're not having a problem with a boy!"

"It's none of your business!"

"Aha!"

She looked away and touched one finger to her nose. Funny, the tiny communications that can absolutely dissolve you: for years she'd had that habit of touching her nose whenever I hurt her feelings.

My anger vanished in a rush of memories—whenever I'd felt friendless, or my parents had seemed unfair, Laura had *been there* for me.

"Hey, I'm having a fascinating summer," I said with a softness that meant I was sorry, "and I'm going to be one of the world's great bridesmaids!"

I hugged her. She hugged me back.

"If you need a shoulder to cry on, mine is always available, Ginny."

A few minutes later, alone downstairs in the kitchen, I watched the steaming milk in a Teflon pot, and I wondered whether Laura had felt about Alan in the beginning the way I now felt about Hal.

Chapter Six

On the car ride to the beach Saturday night, Pam and I up front, Veronica, her guitar, and Rose in back, a Plymouth Duster with a bad case of acne shot alongside us, packed with alien males yelling and waving from the open windows.

"Hey, baby! How you doin', beautiful! WHO-OO-EEE!"

The Duster gunned ahead, disappearing in a blast of speed.

I knew Hal would never behave like those barbarians. Or did I?

In the parking lot behind the sand dunes, we met the other girls and guys. Thermos jugs, blankets, plastic hampers full of food were lugged to a spot where huge driftwood logs lay in the sand a hundred yards from the pounding surf.

No sign of Hal and Rita.

A dozen voices yammered at once, some singing along with the radio that was playing.

"Driftwood for the fire, dummy!"

"I wanna cook the burgers!"

"I wanna cook the cook!"

"The guy's brain is turning into Kool-Whip!"

"Can't you see long tentacles dripping blood coming up out of the sand?"

"Somebody switch him off, will ya?"

The sun was down, the ocean dark, no clouds, a few stars. A curly-haired boy lit a match to the driftwood we had pulled between the two logs. Flames danced.

Where was Hal?

"Do you think it's wrong," Pam asked, eyes on the curly-haired boy nursing the fire, "if I date other boys while Bert's away?"

We were wrapping aluminum foil around the potatoes and cobs of corn to be laid in the fire.

"I don't know, Pam, I've never dated just one guy like you do Bert."

"Well, it makes so so mad that he hasn't written. My father says if I ever get married, the way I act, it wouldn't last a month. I'm too intense, he says. Am I too intense, Ginny?"

Before I could answer her, the curly-haired boy touched her shoulder. "Help me with the hamburgers, Pam?"

She nudged me playfully, winking as she joined him. I stared into the fire. A long-legged freckled boy dropped into Pam's place beside me.

"My name's Mark. I saw your—"

"Excuse me!" I interrupted him and jumped to my feet.

Hal had appeared in the distance, Rita poised lightly in his arms as he moved bare-foot through the sand.

Had Hal seen me sitting with Mark?

The effortless way he carried her, his feet kicking little showers of sand, his shoulders, muscular and broad, rocking slightly with her weight, effortlessly with her weight, effortless yet protective, made me feel I didn't have any right to enter their world.

There was a quality of mystery, of the unknown, clinging to Hal and Rita. To one side of them the moon lifted its enormous orange face over the black silhouette of a tanker on the rim of the sea.

Then Rita called out my name and waved.

Hal's face wore a quizzical expression as I came toward them. What was he thinking?

"I know you two have met, but you haven't

been properly introduced. Ginny Barnes, Hal Stone. Ta-da!"

We nodded. His eyes sparkled at me. I tried to sparkle right back at him.

"Hello."

"Hi, Hal."

From the other side of the fire, Veronica called "Hi!" to Hal as he set Rita down beside me on a blanket facing the flames.

"Ginny, your bikini is fabulous," Rita said. "Don't you think so, Hal?"

"I'm allergic to bikinis," Hal said wryly. "Every time I see one, my eyes break out."

"Hey, we need a quarterback!" a guy's voice bellowed as a weird glow-in-the-dark football came whipping toward us. Hal snatched it out of the air.

Rita and I sat watching the guys and girls run, pass, and block the strange bright football spinning back and forth like a meteor.

Hal leaped high for a pass. Veronica grabbed his arm as he caught the ball, tagging him, and the two of them laughed. She was almost his height. They looked wonderful together, flames on one side of them, moonlight on the other. Mentally I scratched her eyes out.

"Thanks for asking us, Ginny. It's beautiful here, and great for Hal. He spends so much time ferrying me around, he hardly meets anybody."

He has now, I thought bitterly, while Veronica sprinted with the fluorescent football and Hal tagged her.

"I told him your idea, a rainbow on one wall of his room. Got any other good ideas, Ginny?"

"As a matter of fact, I thought of hanging colored fishnet with seashells and stuff."

I also thought of hanging Veronica.

"Who's for a swim?" Hal shouted.

A rush of guys and girls followed Hal down to the waves. He hurtled ahead of them and dived headlong into a wave.

Rita's eyes were gleaming with pleasure. "Go ahead, Ginny! I'm fine here."

I never swam at night, but this time, impulsively, I raced toward the ocean.

The moon was momentarily drowned in inky clouds, the waves darker, more frightening than I had expected. The other kids, stroking ahead, disappeared. A wall of black water swept toward me—I panicked.

A breaking wave swept my legs out from under me. Tumbling blindly, I thrashed at the water. Particles of sand stung my eyes; the violent surf threw me forward, choking me; and the hard slope of sand struck my body like a huge fist.

Shaking, gasping, I pulled myself out of the foaming water. I straightened out my breathing and went toward the fire.

"Was it fun, Ginny? I couldn't see you."

I toweled myself dry and tried to appear calm. "I didn't get very far."

"I bet it was exciting."

I couldn't admit I had been scared to death. "I guess it was sort of exciting."

"Before my accident, I used to swim out at night sometimes, but I never got over being terrified."

Rita sounded so sincere, she punctured—without intending to—my phony pose.

"Terrified just about describes me, too," I admitted.

"Some people—Hal is one—get a kick out of being scared, taking risks."

"How do your parents feel about it?"

Rita's large liquid eyes reflected the firelight as she stared away from me, looking out across the sweep of ocean toward the distant curve of land south of us, where the lighthouse at Castle Point sent its searchlight around and around.

"I'd rather not talk about my parents." She

wrenched the words out, and they seemed like a gate closing between us.

Then she shook her head and shoulders, the way a cat shakes water off its fur, and regained her bubbly spirit. "What's funny is, with all the dangerous things Hal does, *he* worries about *me*!"

"Look, they're coming back!"

Sprinting up from the edge of the sea, wet bodies glistening, the gang of girls and boys charged across the sand toward the fire and burst around us, laughing, chattering.

Hal was not among them. Nor Veronica.

Pam and the curly-haired boy were last to arrive. She sank down, exhausted; the boy disappeared. Kids were screeching and bellowing as they stuffed their mouths with broiled hamburgers and snatched hot corn and potatoes out of the fire.

"I wish Bert was here," Pam whispered pathetically.

I knew she needed me to say something kind, but I guess I wanted her to recognize that I had needs, too.

Rita's head was turned toward the ocean. Calmly she asked, "Was Hal swimming alone?"

Pam shook her head. "He was way out, Veronica too."

An image of Veronica's long blond hair sinking down, down, down, attached to her scalp, gave me a moment of evil pleasure.

"She's coming out of the water!"

Veronica dragged herself up the beach, alone, and presented us with a limp smile.

A moment later, Hal reappeared from the sea, his thick hair swept back around his head like a glistening helmet, and he loped toward the fire just in time to see the boy named Mark hand Rita and me paper plates with hamburgers. Mark cozily folded his long frame down beside me so that his knee was touching mine.

"What's for din-din?" Hal shouted, then glanced at Mark and me and veered away from us toward the other side of the fire, where Veronica was toweling her shoulders and arms, twisting her hips in a provocative way. At first I thought Hal had reacted to Mark and me so close together, but I changed my mind when I saw how he seemed to enjoy Veronica's little games.

And my heart sank when I saw Hal walking with Veronica toward the parking lot, but they quickly returned with his guitar case.

The two of them began strumming their guitars and singing; it seemed as if the whole world, narrowed down to a dozen or so kids around a fire, was focused on the music and words that came from Hal and Veronica.

> Don't ever let me go,
> Love will have no meaning,
> If you leave me,
> Baby, don't you know
> How much you need me?

"They sound like they've been singing together for years. . . ."

"Are they dating?"

"Boy, they make a pair!"

Rita, eyes closed, hummed the music. Other kids joined in. Everybody clapped except me. The two guitars and the two voices moved on to a second song.

I couldn't stand it.

Easing up quickly from the blanket, I slipped away toward the ripples of moon-washed surf. *Don't go, you dope! You're prettier than Veronica, and nicer; go back and make him know you like him!*

The two voices trailed after me. Faster and faster I put the voices behind me, put my dreams of a romance with Hal behind me, and then, when I thought no one could see, I broke into a run.

And I didn't stop until the distant blaze of the driftwood fire looked like a twinkling orange star, so far away I couldn't see any of the kids, as if I were deserted on a strange planet.

Maybe because I felt so isolated, the sea, the rush and tumble and retreat of the waves, sounded friendly for the first time that night.

The sound of the water was like all the human beings on earth—how many billions?—breathing in and out at the same time, and little by little my loneliness washed away.

I closed my eyes and cried a little, a sweet kind of crying.

For a fraction of a second, I wasn't just a teenaged kid who couldn't get the boy she wanted, I was a fat-legged two year old, watching, listening as the hiss and glisten of the ocean carried me out of myself.

> Come home to me,
> My house beside the sea,
> Where you and I will be
> In love again.

Without even realizing it, I was singing the words of an old song my parents often played.

Something touched my shoulder. I jumped about ten feet.

"Sorry if I scared you."

"You didn't scare me. My hair always turns white when someone taps me on the shoulder."

The moonlight, streaming down from behind me, gave a cold glow to Hal's tousled hair and glinted on the silver ring as he combed his fingers through the tangles of his hair.

He wasn't breathing hard, but I knew he had been running.

"I guess you didn't like our singing," Hal said.

He sounded not nearly so sure of himself, which puzzled me.

I turned my profile to him and stared out across the moon-drenched waves. "You and Veronica were great," I said, suppressing any hint of bitterness, "but I had something to think about by myself."

A brusque, defensive note slid into his voice. "You want me to leave you alone?"

After a long pause, I murmured, "I guess that's up to you."

The long shoulder of a wave swung toward the beach, foam spitting off the crest, and tons of water pounded at the sand.

I took a step away from him, a slow step, hoping and hoping that he wouldn't turn to go.

"That song you were singing. . . ." He laid the words out like smooth, round stones.

"It's ancient."

"Some of that old music was great."

"Nat King Cole sang it. My dad has all his records."

"You like the oldies?"

"Some. Frank Sinatra."

"Perry Como."

"Bing Crosby."

"Rosemary Clooney."

"The Andrews Sisters."

We laughed, and our eyes flicked and touched and jumped away like startled cats.

The air had been dead, but now a warm wind blew inland, and gusts of sand hit our ankles. The waves struck harder, it seemed, at the beach, thudding again and again.

Silent, we moved along the shore, our backs to the distant spark of light that was our beach fire.

Moonlight made a million brilliant bits of silver on the waves. Way out where the sky and sea connected, there were specks of light from an invisible boat, with invisible human beings on it.

People talk about everybody having a soul and stuff, and usually I'm not very sure what my soul is and how it's different from the rest of me, but walking in that place with Hal beside me, even though we weren't holding hands or anything, just being together, in step with each other, no houses, no cars or trucks, just bare feet, bare stars, a bare moon, I kind of had a feeling my soul was the main thing.

"How about a swim?" Hal's voice broke the mood.

"I don't think so."

"Don't you like to swim?"

"Sure."

"It'll make you feel better."

"I feel OK."

"No, you don't."

That remark got me annoyed, and I blurted out, "I don't like swimming at night."

"Scared?"

"I just don't feel like swimming."

We were silent again, but only for a moment.

"Hey, Ginny," he said, his voice mellow, and it was the first time, the very, very first time I had ever heard him speak my name, "if you were afraid of swimming and if you were also a flirt, I could make a great pun."

What did he mean, if I was a flirt?

"OK," he said. "What do you call a hen who is a coward *and* a flirt?"

I couldn't keep a few drops of self-defensive

sarcasm out of my voice. "A hen who is a coward and a flirt?"

"A chicken coquette!"

I stared blankly at him.

"Get it? A coquette is a flirt. Chicken *co-quette* instead of chicken *croquette*. You never ate chicken croquettes?"

"It's a rotten joke," I said harshly. "You think I'm a flirt, don't you?"

"No, I don't," he said mildly.

"Then why did you think of it, if it wasn't in your mind already?"

He threw up his hands in exasperation. "Come on, it was just a joke."

"Oh, sure. And who was I flirting with? You think I was flirting with *you*?"

"I didn't say that!"

"I didn't need you to follow me here and make jokes that make me feel worse than I was already feeling!"

"I came because Rita asked me. She was worried about you."

Hot tears came streaming out of my eyes; I couldn't stop them, a dammed-up river of tears.

"Ginny, I'm sorry, I didn't realize you had something real heavy bothering you."

His look of concern, brows knitted, lips pulled together, made the tears flow even faster. It was as if I started crying out of sheer frustration, and then the crying caught hold of something deeper inside me, something I hardly understood.

And before I knew what was happening, Hal kind of touched my shoulder, to be comforting, I guess, a kind of confused and alarmed look in his eyes. I couldn't stop crying; the tears kept coming and coming. Almost accidentally his arm came around me and my arms around him, and he held me tight against him, and he kissed me on the mouth. The strength drained out of me, and my arms fell away from him, only my mouth clinging to his.

"I'm sorry!" he burst out, pulling away from me suddenly, flustered.

"You're *sorry*?"

"Look, I didn't mean—it just happened—I didn't mean to grab—to kiss you."

Ice-cold I asked, "What *did* you mean?"

"You were—you were crying, and I felt—sorry for you."

"You felt *sorry* for me? You creep!"

It had been so beautiful, for a brief moment, and I was enraged that he didn't realize something so *significant* had been happening with us. What possible reason could he have had for pulling away, except that when he kissed me he just didn't like the way I kissed?

"You—you—you jerk!" I shouted at him. "Don't ever speak to me again!"

I ran from him, back toward the fire, toward Pam and Rita and Mark and Veronica and all the others with their glances and their questions, getting myself ready to look so *together* that absolutely no one would suspect I had just gone through the worst and the best moments of my life.

Chapter Seven

I walked for hours, my head spinning, as it had been for several days, the air motionless, the clouds looking like pots of cold oatmeal. It had been raining earlier, and drops of water were still slipping from the leafy trees. I could see the train station, people climbing into the railroad cars that were headed north toward Rivertown, families mostly and some couples, probably excited about seeing a new movie or show. I envied them, I even envied the fat little old lady who came running to catch the train at the last minute, her arms full of packages.

I envied them because they all had a place to go. I'd been miserable ever since the beach party.

Yes, I could have called Rita. I should have

called Rita. I wanted to call Rita. I didn't call Rita.

Not after what had happened with Hal that night on the beach.

I remembered how furious I had felt as I approached Rita and Pam and the gang of kids at the fire. Some of the kids had already scattered into couples, walking, sitting on the dunes, holding hands. Others, like Veronica, were still singing, and two couples were playing touch football with that green fluorescent thing. I was glad to see that Rita, Pam, Rose, Mark, and the curly-haired boy were talking and laughing near the bonfire; I was glad for Rita.

"Hal find you?" Rita had asked.

"Sure. Thanks, Rita. But I was fine."

She and the others cast their eyes along the stretch of beach where I had been with Hal.

"I don't see him."

"He wanted to take a swim."

My guess was correct; a little while later Hal emerged from the ocean, all smiles, and dried his body at the fire. I thought for sure he would make a big play for Veronica, but to my surprise, Hal had merely murmured a few words to Rita and then announced, "We're heading home. Got an early day tomorrow."

Hal hoisted Rita easily into his arms. She blew me a kiss. I avoided Hal's eyes and refused to utter a word in his direction. He took a step forward with Rita, stopped, turned toward me, and said, sort of to everyone, but I knew it was directed at me:

"The early nerd catches the worm, as long as you don't put all your spilled milk in one basket!"

And then they left, across the sand and into the dark.

That night I had gone to bed depressed, seesawing between scalding tears and visions of Hal and the gallows with a knotted rope around his neck.

And for the next few days I played the scenes on the beach with Hal over and over in my head. Did he kiss me only because he felt sorry? Was I absolutely sure he pulled away because the kiss was crummy? "The early nerd catches the worm," he had said. Was he calling me a worm and himself a nerd for catching me? Or himself a worm at the mercy of a nerd like me? Or was he just trying to reach out with a little humor? Come on, Ginny, cut out all the analyzing!

That's why I decided to walk and walk and walk, out past the train station, then onward up the last low hill of houses that blocked the view of Rivertown.

Beyond the distant metal-and-glass office buildings of Rivertown lay a series of wrinkled hills, and the dark clouds over the hills looked ready to burst open.

I felt I was about to burst open too, but what kind of rain, I wondered, would come out of *me*? No gentle summer shower, that was for sure.

Turning my footsteps back toward home, I kicked an aluminum can someone had lazily dropped. I was angry and confused as I stepped into the street—a truck horn blared at me, and the bumper of the truck almost removed an inch of my waistline.

If I get hit by a truck, it'll be *his* fault! And just because of him I haven't called Rita! I thought about how I wanted to continue being friends with her. Impulsively I dashed into a phone booth and dialed their number, planning to invite Rita to go with me into Rivertown and visit one of the art museums, and planning to hang up if the person who answered the phone was you-know-who.

No one answered the phone.

I struck out toward home. The blast of a motorcycle horn froze my feet on the yellow line. You want to get home in one piece, Ginny, get your act together!

I concentrated on sidewalks, gutters, stop signs, and traffic, at least *tried* to concentrate. Next thing I knew—I did it unconsciously, I swear—I was walking past Mrs. Harley's house, a good quarter of a mile in the wrong direction from my house, and the sight of the Jackson Construction truck threw me into a panic. I would have died if Hal had seen me and thought I had *purposely* walked past where he was working.

That's why I darted across the street, hurried down the block, swung around the corner, and continued, almost at a jog, for another half block before I breathed a sigh of relief.

Then a car honked, one of those deep, annoying car horns that remind you of Dracula gargling.

Well, I knew it wasn't me they were honking at, since I was striding along the sidewalk, not the gutter, but the honking continued, and I shot a glance behind me.

What I saw was painted in swirls of jungle green and yellow and earthy browns and black, camouflage colors all over the fenders and doors.

And the person honking at the wheel, driving about as fast as I was walking, was Hal.

I looked away as if he didn't exist and kept my feet, somehow, in spite of the momentary weakness that flooded the muscles, slapping against the sidewalk.

"Hey, Ginny, stop a minute!"

I kept walking.

He kept following.

I turned, purposely, down a one-way street.

He followed me, driving in reverse, and when I crossed kitty-corner to the next street over, I saw that the other side of his weirdo car was painted in some sort of ocean camouflage, wavy streaks of navy blue, turquoise, gray, white, green. Ugh!

"Ginny, wait!" he called again.

I hurried under the fire-red neon sign that said Acropolis Diner and hopped up three steps and went inside, passing a bright blue and red machine that promised, for a quarter, to produce a "biorhythm chart," which would predict what kind of a day I would have. I didn't need a machine to tell me.

Heart pounding, seated at the counter with my back to the glass door, I attempted to read the menu, while a gum-chewing waitress laid out a napkin for me.

Moments later, with a glass of soda in front of me, I heard someone clear his throat loudly on the seat beside me. "Operator," he said, "I'd like to make a person-to-person call to Ginny Barnes."

Without a word, I spun out of my seat, check in hand, dropped the check and a dollar on the glass plate in front of the cashier, and leaped down the three steps of the diner, feet flashing toward home, all in a blur of motion, though I knew Hal was right behind me because he called out, "You might as well stop and listen. I'm not about to go away, Ginny!"

Raindrops, dark and fat, began printing patterns on the sidewalk. I quickened my pace, but Hal jogged easily alongside me.

"I don't want to talk to you!" I clipped the words at him and raced ahead.

Almost immediately Hal caught up with me, but he hardly got a word out before the sky turned into a sieve and sheets of rain plunged against our bodies.

"I WANT TO APOLOGIZE!" he yelled at the top of his voice.

"GO AHEAD!" I yelled back at him.

Hal stared at me, water streaming down our faces, plastering our hair and our clothes to our skins, drumming on the parked cars.

"My feet are drowning," he said. "How about yours?"

The silly, handsome, mischievous grin on his face hooked itself into me.

"Glug glug," I answered.

We both laughed so that you couldn't tell which of us the laugh belonged to.

People passed us on the sidewalk, hiding their heads under umbrellas—first a tiny brown one, then a clear plastic one, then a black one with a scalloped edge. Each pair of eyes swung in our direction as if they thought we were pretty peculiar taking a shower with our clothes on.

"I told Rita what happened on the beach, and Rita told me that you were absolutely right about one thing. I was definitely a jerk."

"But a *nice* jerk," I corrected him.

"A nice *wet* jerk," he added, grinning.

"*Two* wet jerks," I said, meeting the friendliness of his smile with my own.

A silence in the trees and on the pavement and the hoods of cars made us aware that the rain was suddenly ending. The air, washed clean, smelled of grass and earth and wet leaves.

"I really didn't want to make you feel bad."

"I know."

"OK, as long as you know."

"Thanks, Hal."

"And any time you happen to need an apology or two, don't hesitate to give me a ring—at home, on the job, I'm always available for apologies."

I had a queer feeling that Hal was saying he wanted to see me again, but how was I supposed to be sure? I almost said, "Well, so long, Hal, it sure was nice getting soaked to the skin with you," but I bit my tongue because the words sounded too sarcastic.

Instead, I said, "Did you have any day in mind when you'd like to apologize again?"

"Okayyyyy!" he drawled, and I couldn't figure whether he was being serious or mocking, until he added, "How about Saturday afternoon, say three o'clock?"

"Great!" I said, and immediately regretted my enthusiasm because his enthusiasm definitely sounded less enthusiastic than mine.

"Got to get back to work at Mrs. Harley's," he said. "See you Saturday!"

Upstairs in my room, no more than twenty minutes later, one thought kept running through my mind: Hal Stone, you sure are hard to figure out!

I flung open my bedroom window, breathed the late summer air, and wondered what the neighbors would say if I suddenly shouted at the top of my voice, "HAPPY BIRTHDAY, EVERYBODY!"

Chapter Eight

I should have been walking on air, but instead, in the days that followed, I kept analyzing how it had happened that Hal and I had made a date.

He had said, "I'm always available for apologies," which had sounded like he was asking me to go out.

But now I wasn't so sure.

Maybe when I had answered, "Do you have any particular day in mind?" it had kind of *embarrassed* him into making a date with me.

On the other hand, he could easily have said something slick, to get off the hook, "Just make an appointment with my secretary," or maybe, "I'm sorry, you'll have to get a doctor's certificate saying you're healthy enough to survive two Hal Stone apologies in a row."

Anyway, as Saturday approached, I got more and more nervous, and I practically bounced off the walls making preparations to impress him.

For example, library books lay scattered on my bed: *The Art of Hang Gliding, Scuba Diver's Bible, Mysteries of Karate,* and (double ugh!) *Snakes For Everyone.* Reading them was a trip I wasn't sure I wanted to take.

Also, since Hal was so joke-oriented, I pored over a book entitled *Jokes For Every Occasion.*

And I bought a sundress the color of a dandelion.

"Discreet, yet sexy," the elderly saleswoman had persuaded me.

Come on, Ginny, you've had plenty of dates before. Don't make this into a Broadway musical! I told myself.

Meanwhile, on the skin between my thumb and forefinger, a very nervous and stubborn rash appeared.

On Saturday morning I soaked in a bubble bath for an hour. Then I painted my toenails and fingernails a color called Incandescent Ecstasy. Picking a perfume almost drove me to despair. Would Hal prefer the scent of Dark Desire or Summer Spice?

As the hands of the clock moved toward three, I arranged myself in the new sundress, wooden clogs, copper loop earrings, and I dabbed the back of my ears, my temples, my throat, the insides of my wrists with Dark Desire.

After a long, intense self-examination, I whipped off my clothes and reappeared in front of the mirror wearing jeans, a green cotton shirt, and sandals with sculpted heels.

Sorry, wrong number.

How about my minilength T-shirt dress, hip wrapped and bloused a little with a dressy belt, and open-toed pumps?

Somehow the outfit didn't set off any fireworks.

Back to the yellow sundress? The blue with the V-neck? The jeans?

"Ginny! Phone call!"

The voice on the phone was Hal's.

"Ginny, I forgot to ask you to bring a bathing suit." He sounded very mature over the phone. "And a towel."

"What are we doing?"

"It's a surprise."

A bathing suit and towel did not sound at all like my blue V-neck with cap sleeves.

I finally chose my pink poplin shirt and pleated white tennis shorts and woven leather flats.

Downstairs Mom and Dad awarded me their best thousand-watt smiles of encouragement.

"Where did you meet this boy Hal?" Mom asked.

"At Mrs. Harley's house."

"He must be pretty unusual." Dad patted me on the shoulder.

"Why?"

"I've never seen you so jittery."

"I'm not jittery, Dad. I just wasn't sure what to wear."

"Just as long as you know how terrific you are," Dad added.

For his sake, I told myself how terrific I was, but I couldn't have passed a lie detector test for beans.

And I decided to wait for Hal downstairs in the basement playroom, where no one would see how high-strung I was.

When I opened the basement door, the voices of Laura and Alan resounded from below.

"You're making a mountain out of a mole-hill!"

"I'm trying to be honest about my feelings, Alan Alston."

"Honest?"

The anger in their voices upset me. What could they be arguing about only two weeks before their wedding day?

"We should talk about it, Alan."

"Don't throw *should* at me!"

I closed the basement door and escaped upstairs, feeling shaken.

If Laura and Alan had troubles, what was in store for Hal and me? Alan was a sweetheart, an easygoing guy, not nearly so complicated as Hal seemed.

I changed from my pink poplin shirt and tennis shorts and woven leather sandals into my tailored jeans and orange, raglan-sleeved polo shirt.

"Your date is here, Ginny!"

"Be right down, Mom!"

My tailored jeans and raglan sleeves and woven flats went flying.

I descended the steps, clomping away in my clogs, and catching a final, fairly satisfying look, in the wall mirror halfway down, of a dandelion sundress, discreet, yet sexy. At the same time I repeated to myself some of the jokes I had memorized with the idea of fitting them into our conversation.

What's a teenager? The only member of the animal kingdom that can eat its heart out without affecting its appetite. How do you heal a pig with a sore throat? Give it some oinkment. What's the final proof that insanity is hereditary? So many parents get it from their children.

But the memory of Hal's kiss that night on the beach made me feel like an actress who is about to go onstage and realizes at the last minute that she has studied the wrong part.

Chapter Nine

Silence is a special thing, the silence of two people in a sailboat, the silence of the ocean slapping the white curve of the hull, the silence of wind against the white edges of the sails, the silence in a sky as fragile as blue tissue paper, and the silence between the words that we spoke to each other now and then.

"Your first time in a sailboat?"

"Uh-huh."

"I started when I was eight."

"What were you like?"

"At eight?" He shrugged and squinted into the sun. "The usual."

I felt like telling him he certainly wasn't the usual, but I was afraid of breaking the mood, so instead I let my arm hang over the edge of the boat, and I trailed my fingers in the water.

"What were *you* like at eight?" he countered.

"The usual," I said, suppressing a grin.

"Somehow I don't think either of us is the usual," he said as if he had read my mind, and he flashed a smile that made my heart skip.

At that moment the wind changed direction, and the edge of the mainsail began flapping, the boat slowing; Hal swung the tiller and shouted, "Duck your head, Ginny!" just in time for me to get my head down as the long aluminum boom attached to the bottom of the sail swung across the width of the boat. The sail snapped out tight against the line that Hal held in his free hand, and the hull scudded farther and farther from the marina where Hal's Uncle Jeff kept the boat. Behind us the masts of the docked boats swayed in the light wind.

"I can guess what you were like when you were eight," he said in a teasing voice.

"I bet you know me better than I know myself," I said, making my best effort to inject some charm into my mocking remark.

The sailboat seemed like a slender, white-winged creature, carrying the two of us on its back across the rippled surface of the bay toward places I had never been.

"*You* were the kind of eight year old," Hal drawled lazily, one muscular arm hooked over the tiller as he leaned back against the stern of the boat, "who was always raising her hand in class to answer the teacher's questions and never letting anybody copy from her. You always looked so pretty and sweet, but if a boy pushed you or pulled your hair, you'd give him a kick that he'd never forget."

"And you, when *you* were eight years old, Hal Stone," I said, pretending to be stern, "you were always throwing spitballs when the teacher's back was turned, but you were very kind to animals and wouldn't let the other boys squash caterpillars in front of you, and whenever you teased a girl or knocked her books out of her arms, she always knew you were a real skunk but definitely not a *mean* skunk."

We laughed, our faces thrown back toward the sky. I felt very close to Hal, although we weren't even within touching distance, and when he looked at me, his hazel eyes wide open, his mouth parted, the sail casting a shadow across the strong planes of his face, I had to look away for fear of revealing everything in me.

"How do you catch a squirrel?" I shot at him glibly, covering up the overpowering feelings surging inside me.

He furrowed his brow dutifully. "How?"

"You climb up a tree and act like a nut."

Solemn, he said, "That's a funny joke."

"Then why aren't you laughing?"

"My tonsils are laughing. See?" He stretched his mouth wide. I peered down his throat. Our faces were close. We chuckled. But the expression in his dark-lashed eyes was solemn and serious.

"Ginny?"

"Yes?"

"Forget it."

Something was troubling him, and I knew—hoped—he would share it with me.

"I like the sound of my name when you say it" was what I wanted to tell him, but I didn't have the courage.

Behind us the wake of our boat curled in a long white tail of foam, and ahead of us the changing colors of the sea were like drifting scarves of olive and jade and blue. Once in a while our eyes would meet, shyly. What passed between us I couldn't explain in words; we weren't actually touching each other, and we weren't talking, yet we seemed to be communicating something deep and wonderful.

We passed the lighthouse and sailed toward a tiny island—mostly rocks and scrubby trees. As we drew nearer, I could make out the new cones on the stunted evergreens and the arching stems of the wild oats rooted in the sand dunes between the rocks, and I lay my head back against the deck of our sailboat, letting the rays of the evening sun sink deep into me.

As we glided past the little island, Hal began whistling, not just ordinary whistling, but trills and unusual vibrations in a soft, slow tune, a tune with sadness and happiness in it.

"Let's never go back!" Those words whispered inside me, as the film of a movie unwound in my imagination.

"We can live on that island!" I imagined Hal saying. "I can build a hut and fish for our food."

"Just the two of us!"

"We'll have to get married," he would assert firmly.

"Yes, that would be for the best," I would agree demurely.

"In the winter we could sail south. They'd never find us."

"The only trouble is," I would say, feeling a

bit brazen as I reached toward him and kissed his chin, "I hate fish. . . ."

Hal's whistling brought me back to reality, the tune jumping from the slow melody to a fast sailor's jig. All you could see of the land behind us was a dark fringe like the stubble of a beard.

"Want to take a swim?"

I looked around at the vast ocean. Who knew what could be way out here, I thought. My mind flew back to the *Scuba Diver's Bible*, visions of sharks, barracuda, killer whales, sting rays. According to the book, if you are in the water and you sighted a shark, the most important thing was *don't freeze*—just keep your eye on the shark and keep retreating. I shivered. Ginny, say hello to your friendly neighborhood tiger shark.

"I don't think so, Hal." I tried to sound relaxed.

"Just as well," he said, giving no clue if he was disappointed. "Be dark soon anyway, and I think we might hit some weather."

Some *weather*? My throat tightened at the way he said that. He turned the tiller, the boom swung, and the sails flapped, then bellied out tighter. In a few minutes the sky began clouding over, the wind picked up, the ocean was no longer so calm.

"Better put on this life jacket." You could see from the set of his jaw and the way he combed his fingers through his hair that the whipping wind and the waves beginning to splash against the hull of the boat were a challenge he loved.

I gulped inwardly, where no one could see or hear the gulp, a gulp that definitely represented years of first-rate cowardice.

"If you insist," I said, hoping he didn't notice the neon yellow streak that was flashing on and off all the way down my spine.

Chapter Ten

He didn't call on Sunday.

He didn't call on Monday.

Nor Tuesday. Nor Wednesday.

Etcetera.

AARGH!

School started nine days after my sail with Hal, and still no call.

Senior year, at least—ha! What good was senior year if Hal didn't call?

For the first few days after our date, I hung around the house, expecting the phone to ring any minute. And when I was out shopping or something, I worried that no one would be there to answer his call.

I even thought of investing in one of those recording gadgets that answer the phone with your own voice on tape: "Hello, this is Ginny

Barnes. I'm so sorry to miss your call that it practically makes me ill. So when you hear the beep, please, *please*, leave your name and number so I can call you right back."

I couldn't understand why I didn't hear from him. Our date had gone so well. Almost perfectly—and the almost was hardly an almost at all, at least in my humble opinion.

The only thing that might have bothered Hal was when the wind got really strong and the sailboat rocked and yawed, up and down, waves slamming against the hull, up and down, up and down, and my stomach went berserk, and I got sick in the Atlantic Ocean. Not exactly the most romantic way to arrive at the marina.

I staggered off the boat and onto the dock, and my legs wobbled like wilted celery, but I was able to see, at least I think I was, that Hal wasn't the least bit embarrassed by my misadventure.

From the boat yard we had driven to a Chinese restaurant where we invented dumb jokes about egg foo yung ("It looks too old to be *young*") and chow mein ("No one eats *chow* like this in Maine").

And when we got home and sat for a moment in Hal's car, I could sense with every atom in my body that he wanted to kiss me.

He took me to the door of my house. As I turned the knob, at the last moment, he said, "Wait, Ginny!" and he leaned his face toward my face. I closed my eyes, lips quivering, and felt his finger rub against my cheek.

"Just some dirt on your cheek," he said softly, then jogged to his car and gunned away.

So he didn't kiss me, but every particle in me could sense that we both had had a beautiful time together, so why wasn't he calling me for another date?

Asking Rita's advice might have made me feel better. She and I spent hours and hours browsing in different stores for decorating ideas for Hal's room. But I didn't want to make her feel I was using her to get close to Hal. I really liked her. I mean, apart from him.

At school Hal and I passed each other twice in the hallway outside my psychology class, also at the phone booth near the principal's office, also in the lunchroom, also on the street. And every time, except one, he was with a different girl, and I was with a different boy; and every time, except one, we waved to each other and kept going in our own directions, although I really *yearned* to stop and grab him by the shoulders and shake him.

It was what you might call a heavy week.

And Pam, that very week, had a terrible argument in the lunchroom with Bert. Over nothing. She said she hated her nose. He said he liked her nose. She said he should admit he really hated her nose. He said she had a beautiful Greek nose like his grandma. She cried and called him a liar. He went stomping away with half a crummy cafeteria frankfurter crushed in his fist.

"Ginny," Pam appealed, "why am I so stupid and sensitive?"

"I'm the same way, Pam, believe me."

"But you're not unhappy!"

"Maybe I just don't show it."

The week was also particularly rough because my family was getting ready for Laura's wedding to Alan, and I was supposed to be thrilled. Well, I was, but I would have been more thrilled if Hal was coming. Why didn't I invite him? No guts.

The night before the wedding, Laura knocked on my door and came in and hugged me as if she never wanted to let go.

"Ginny, I feel like I'm about to jump off a cliff."

She actually looked scared, and I felt a stab of sorrow that we were losing each other.

"Ginny, I don't know if I can make him happy."

And yet the next day, the day of the wedding, when Alan slipped the ring on her finger in our living room, which was crowded with guests, Laura looked calm and serene. And when we rained rice on them as they jumped in their car to go shooting off to a honeymoon cabin in the Florida Keys, Laura seemed so sure of herself, laughing, smiling.

As for me, I became less and less sure. The next five days at school repeated the same pattern with Hal. We'd see each other, he'd be with some girl, I'd be with some boy, and we'd smile cheerily and wave.

The fact is, my being with so many different boys was understandable because I was a senior and a lot of boys knew me. Although I never had the number of dates I remember Laura having, there were always boys hanging around and walking me places.

Whereas Hal, well, he'd just recently transferred to Jefferson High, and you'd think he could have had the decency, after how close we had seemed on our date, not to flaunt himself with every girl he met!

But there was one occasion in school when we did more than just grin and wave to each other, and it was wonderfully horrible.

It happened during change of classes, near the water fountain on the third floor. I was alone. He was alone.

"Ginny!"

"Hi, Hal!"

His eyes opened wide with spontaneous pleasure. I felt myself grinning broadly.

"What do you think the chances are an earthquake will destroy this building?"

His eyes were dancing.

"Are you expecting an earthquake?" I asked, a little stiff at first, because I'd been feeling neglected by him, but warming to his warmth.

"The amount of homework they give in this school, they deserve an earthquake, at least a six on the Richter scale."

It was the way his mouth curved, I guess, and the way he lazily leaned his shoulder against the plaster wall and the way his nose wrinkled when he grinned that washed away—for the moment at least—my week of confusion and disappointment.

"I guess they went to sharpen us up for the college entrance exams."

"Couldn't we have a small earthquake and get a little less sharpened up?"

"OK," I yielded, "but just a small one."

"I knew you'd agree." He beamed. I found myself hoping he was on the verge of saying why don't we get together? But he only said, "Hey, don't look so serious, Ginny!"

"Was I looking serious? I thought I was smiling."

"Tell you what. You don't want an earthquake, I'll change it to a flood. Just to get rid of the teachers who are boring, OK?"

"That's a deal," I said, chuckling.

"After all, the world is a hopeless mess anyway. What's another flood between friends?" His voice carried a hint of harshness I hadn't heard before.

I guess I felt a little threatened by his cynical attitude—I like to believe the world isn't so bad—and I said defensively, "A lot of people try really hard to make things good. People like Rita, for example."

A sudden bitterness that seemed directed at me flooded his voice. "She shouldn't have to try so hard!"

"What are you snapping at me for?" I snapped.

"I'm not snapping!" he snapped. "I just want Rita to have the best!"

"Well, so do I!"

"You hardly even know her!"

"I guess I know what I don't know without *you* telling me!"

I wanted so badly to slap his face for not

having the least idea how happy I could make him.

"Well, so long, Ginny," he said, without a trace of sarcasm, as if we had just shared a beautiful few minutes, and he held his palm up, facing me, and waved a couple of times like a windshield wiper moving back and forth, and as he strolled away, he added over his shoulder, "It sure has been swell arguing with you."

Chapter Eleven

"Hello, Ginny."

I heard his voice behind me, his voice the way I remembered it from that very first time at Mrs. Harley's house.

"Hello, Hal," I murmured, my face flushing with surprise and embarrassment.

On the movie marquee, *Three Loves*, written in bright letters, flashed on and off. People came streaming from the doors of the theater, hundreds of faces crowded together, here and there a young couple holding hands as if they shared some secret.

"How was the picture?" Hal asked casually.

"*Three Loves*? I haven't seen it yet. I'm waiting for Rita."

"So am I," he said slowly. "She told me

Uncle Jeff was bringing her here to meet me for the seven o'clock show."

"She said the same to me."

We stared at each other, not quite sure how to react. I was still nursing my wounds from our last conversation near the third-floor water fountain.

"Looks like she set it up for us to . . ." Hal let out a whistle, and he stuck his hands in his pockets.

"You think she purposely? . . ."

A young woman wearing a gold-striped uniform opened the middle doors; the line of ticket holders surged into the lobby.

"My guess is, knowing Rita," Hal said, pursing his lips in a sort of pout, which slowly unwound as he spoke into a playful grin, "that she figured her brother is an oversensitive clown who needs a push in the right direction."

I was nodding my head; I had been oversensitive, too.

"Are you nodding your head because you agree I'm oversensitive or because you agree I'm a clown?" Hal asked ominously.

For a moment I thought he was serious and we were about to let loose another swarm of angry words. I stiffened, ready to defend myself, but he suddenly dropped the ominous tone. "Sorry, Ginny. Lately I get uptight over nothing."

"Is that why you didn't ask me for another date after we went sailing?"

The question popped out of my mouth unexpectedly before I could put a lid on it; instantly I regretted asking, because now he would know how much I had wanted him to call me. I squirmed, feeling that my brain was glass and he was staring in at all the dumb, insecure thoughts.

"I guess I didn't ask you because I didn't think you particularly *wanted* me to ask you. Did you want me to?"

I nodded.

"I wasn't sure you had a good time."

"*I* had a great time, Hal."

He buried his fingers in his hair. "I didn't want to ask for a date and get turned down."

I wanted to say, "What does a girl have to do to make you know she likes you?" But instead I said, "Why would I turn you down?"

That look came into his eyes, the look of things hidden. "Why do people do the things they do? A million reasons, I guess."

I lifted my chin toward the movie marquee overhead. "You know, Hal, I hear *Three Loves* is a terrific movie."

His seriousness vanished. "Ginny, would you? . . ."

Laughing, I grabbed his arm.

The tired woman in the glass booth was pushing orange tickets toward a young couple about our age who hurried past the uniformed usherette.

Darkness. Waves of tender music. The movie screen lit up with a long view of green mountains wreathed in mist.

We slipped into two seats in an empty row down front. My heart started beating like a scared bird in a cage because Hal just so naturally slipped his arm around my shoulders and I, without questioning, let my head rest against him.

Afterward I couldn't remember much of the movie, but I did remember the texture of Hal's sleeve against my neck, his fingers and my fingers knitting together, the funny way we kept passing a bucket of popcorn back and forth, and the way we licked our fingers when the bucket was empty.

And when the father in the film died to save his family, I glimpsed a tear on Hal's cheek before he roughly brushed it away.

The only downer was one brief moment on the way out the exit doors into the parking lot, the night sky jammed with stars, when I remarked, "I thought the father was really, really wonderful."

I was completely unprepared for the sarcasm that Hal fired at me. "Oh, yeah, fathers in *movies* are really, really, *wonderful.*"

If there is one thing in this world I hate, it is being scornfully imitated, but before I could retaliate, Hal slipped his arm around my waist, his voice gentle again. "What does a collie eat?"

I shrugged.

"Cauliflower."

I laughed as he opened the car door for me. I was glad I had asked Mom to drop me at the theater instead of driving myself.

"How do you make a Chinese egg roll?" I asked as he slid behind the steering wheel.

"I don't know."

"You *push* it."

Hal honked his horn at a driver who had jumped a red light. Traffic was surprisingly heavy. The lights of passing cars splashed across his profile as he drove. I chewed over the acid remark he had made about fathers. I recalled how Rita had not wanted to discuss her parents. Were Hal's parents the reason he was so sensitive? How come he and Rita were living with their *uncle*? Was that his secret? Or was it some girl he had left behind when he moved who still upset him?

The wheels of Hal's car rubbed against the edge of the curb in front of my house. He turned the engine off.

Our eyes met. We moved toward each other until our lips touched, touched and remained together, with almost no pressure, yet as if nothing could ever separate us, and then, as if by unspoken agreement, we moved apart.

Hours later, alone, snuggled against my pillow, staring at the moon shadows thrown through the window at my wall, I fought against sleep, trying to cling to the powerful sense of Hal's presence.

Chapter Twelve

The weather turned windy a few days after we saw *Three Loves*, and the trees, though still thick with leaves, flapped up and down and whispered and rushed and rustled.

The late September air forced people into sweaters and light jackets, but I didn't mind giving up the summer warmth, because every hour I spent with Hal was a special small universe with no one else in it but us.

When I wasn't with him, the hours dragged, at home, at school, at the First Aid Squad; even redecorating my room didn't grab me.

We dated each other at least twice a week, sometimes Friday and Saturday, sometimes only Friday or only Saturday, and usually we'd meet after school one day a week and stay together until supper time.

I had held hands with and kissed boys quite a few times in my life, and usually I liked it. With Hal, however, it wasn't just holding hands, it wasn't just kissing, it was a whole new feeling.

If we were sitting close to each other or talking, we often just drifted together, each sending an unspoken message that we wanted to kiss, and the meeting of our lips sent a sweet but scary current of excitement into every part of my body.

Sometimes Hal and I walked on the deserted beach near the Coast Guard station, the wind flapping at our clothes, the surf pounding, the sea gulls looping and squealing. And sometimes we wound along the paths of Webster Park, a mile or so north of my house, past the yelling kids playing sandlot baseball, around the artificial lake where white and black ducks paddled. We spent long stretches of time together just holding hands, and occasionally we'd kiss when no one was around.

Nothing we saw together or heard together was ordinary—the hills, birds, grass, the wind rubbing leaves, a road curving away in the distance, a spider's web strung between a fence and a bush—it all seemed new.

It was a time of wonders. I hoped Hal felt the same.

But his feelings seemed to turn on and off, and I was never really sure what I meant to him.

Was I getting across what a great time I had with him and how much I wanted him to keep dating me?

He certainly kept phoning, but when we were together, I was always a little off balance, watching his face, looking for his signals. Sometimes I was certain he felt the way I felt; other times he looked so somber, so distant, like a stranger who didn't care at all.

And why did I quash my desire to ask him what his life was like before we met? Scared to rock the boat, I guess. Especially when the conversation came near anything that had to do with *parents*. Hal clammed right up, and I could see the storm clouds gather on his face.

But for the most part, at least when no one was around, it was beautiful hugs and kisses, long drives in the country, sharing a pizza.

Of course, there was no easy way to see each other after school. I had my first aid meetings and tons of homework, and I had to write to at least six different colleges that interested me. And Hal still worked for his uncle two days a week and went to meetings of his hang-gliding club and took karate instruction.

I did feel a little guilty about not spending enough time with Pam, knowing she and Bert had problems, but I did talk a lot with her in school and on the phone, which was more than she had done for me when she and Bert, way back, had gone so hot and heavy together.

Rita, oddly, in spite of the number of times I phoned her to keep in touch, almost always seemed to be out somewhere with her uncle or at painting classes or life-study drawing classes. I suspected she was trying to give Hal and me the time and space we needed.

As for my sister Laura, she and Alan had returned from their honeymoon and were busy furnishing the house they had rented twenty minutes' drive away. Laura didn't seem wildly happy.

But all I truly cared about was Hal calling to see me and both of us wanting more and more of each other. I went to sleep every night with the memory of his eyes, dark and warm and unpredictable, his thick soft hair that smelled of incense and rain, and the touch of his lips.

It would have been one hundred percent heaven if I didn't continue to see him on the stairs in school with some cute redhead or shoveling mashed potatoes down his throat in the lunchroom nose to nose with a gorgeous blond cheerleader type and waving a yard-wide smile at me as if I should be delighted that he had such nice company for lunch.

I didn't have the guts to walk right over and join him. Yet he always waved in the friendliest way. Still, I felt that if he wanted to be with me all he had to do was say goodbye to whatever girl he was with and come on over. He certainly didn't expect *me* to walk over and sit down with the two of *them*.

This didn't happen every day. Often he was alone, and I went over, or I was alone, and he came over to me.

But if I was with a boy or any of my friends, he would wave or nod and walk right by.

It was a weird game he was playing, or we were playing. I'd be sinking my teeth into a tuna sandwich and making polite conversation with, say, Todd Wilkins, who was pretty nice-looking but didn't interest me one bit, and Hal would go past us all alone, and I would smile, and Hal would smile and walk all the way to the other side of the lunchroom.

And another thing bothered me almost as much. Hal set up this force field around himself whenever he and I were with other people—anyone, Pam, Rita, kids in school; if I had an urge to be affectionate to him in public, his force field would stop me cold. We never discussed it; it just was.

But when we were alone, he was totally different, the force field vanished, and we were always cuddling and snuggling and nestling in each other's arms. So I often thought, "Give him time, Ginny, he'll change, he'll change. He's just very private about his real deep affection."

But it was pretty strange that we seemed so close and still never mentioned his mom or dad. I was dying of curiosity, and once, in the school cafeteria with him, I took a chance and blurted out, "Are your parents coming to see you graduate, Hal?"

"They've got better things to do!" he said and gave me a big, false smile. "Hey, listen, I'll see you later, Ginny, I forgot something!"

And he whizzed out of the cafeteria.

I figured that was his way of telling me to lay off. And it worked.

So things weren't perfect between us, but most of the time, especially when we were alone, the good times were so good.

Like when Hal took me to Silver Falls.

Chapter Thirteen

When we went to Silver Falls, the green in the leaves was giving way to tints of yellow and crimson and copper, but the cold weather had eased up a bit. Dazzling in the sunlight, a silver bow of water curved outward from a rock shelf in a notch of hills before plunging downward at least two hundred feet. We saw it even from the parking lot at the ranger station, and the closer we came along the path marked with wooden Forest Service arrows, the more magnificent the falls appeared, until we were close enough to hear the sound of the water crashing into the stream below.

I reached my face up toward Hal's, but he stiffened and drew away when he saw a couple with a child straggling down the path toward us.

Farther on, the path wound along the bank of the stream, and we followed the loop of glittering water until we came to a place off the path, sheltered from people by low-hanging spruce trees, where we could be alone.

"Thanks, Hal."

"Why?"

"I've always wanted to see the falls this way."

"Your folks never took you here?"

"Oh, sure, but it's different with someone—"

"With someone what?"

Our faces were so close. My cheek grazed his cheek. Our hands seemed to find each other.

"Are you glad we came here?" I asked with hesitation.

His answer was to fold me in his arms and hold me so close I could hardly breathe.

"You're hurting me, Hal."

"I'm sorry." He jumped away, and his face looked so tense, so apologetic.

"Don't take your arms away. Just not so hard."

I slid my hand against his. He relaxed. He kissed my cheek. He kissed my forehead. He kissed my eyes.

"No one ever kissed my eyes," I whispered. He gave me a peculiar look, as if he wasn't sure I had liked it, but I felt too embarrassed to say anything further.

We sat on the grass for a long time, holding each other and staring through a gap in the trees at the water surging into space before its plunge downward.

I broke the silence. "Pam asked me if you and I would like to double-date with her and Bert."

"I'd rather not."

"Any particular reason?"

"I don't like a lot of people."

"I'm a people."

"I mean, well, I'd rather it just be the two of us."

The two of us. That sounded good. So what if Hal didn't ever want to double with other couples? The two of us were more than enough. Or were we? Didn't I really want us to go out with other kids? Didn't I want people to see us together, to be identified as a couple, instead of people thinking we were just casually dating?

"Oh, who cares what people think!" a big strong voice growled inside my head. And a small, weak, but very definite voice answered, "You do, Ginny, baby!"

Well, the first frost of the winter struck hard one night not long after our enchanted time at Silver Falls. The windows in my bedroom were sketched with glistening ice pictures. Water froze in the rain pipes. Icicle daggers hung wickedly from the eaves of the roof. My mother burned the french toast. I single-handedly eradicated my favorite ceramic mug. The battery in my father's car needed a reincarnation. It was not a promising day, except for the promise Hal had made to pick me up at my First Aid Squad meeting. I hoped it would interest him to see where I volunteered.

But when I gave him a tour of the radio set-up, the training room, the emergency equipment, the gleaming red-and-white ambulance with three different kinds of sirens, he stifled a yawn and said, "That's, uh, fascinating, Ginny."

Was I disappointed? Not at all. Well, maybe a little. Maybe a little more than a little. As a matter of fact, every time I tried to talk to Hal about my interests, such as first aid and decorating, his face took on such a wooden expression that I quickly dropped the subject.

What does it mean if the guy you feel closer to than any other you have ever known is totally cold to activities that really turn you on? Well, let's be honest, Ginny, how captivated are *you* by Hal's boa constrictor, his scuba tanks and spear gun, his karate and his hang glider?

Anyway, after we left the First Aid Squad, Hal drove me to Webster Park. Showers of leaves came spinning down from the trees onto our heads and shoulders as we ambled past the young mothers pushing their baby strollers, and the kids kicking a soccer ball.

"I think college will be much better than high school," I said, just to make conversation.

"Me, I don't intend to find out."

"You've got to go to college, Hal!"

"Why?"

"Because you're really bright, and you'd be wasting your intelligence."

"In other words, you think my intelligence has a big enough waist already, so I shouldn't put my brains on a diet."

"I'm serious, Hal!"

"Ginny, you sound like my parents."

That hurt. I turned away.

"I'm sorry, Ginny," he said sincerely, "but the human race'll go down the drain whether I graduate from college or not."

"Why don't you ever talk about your parents?" I blurted out.

"What's the point?"

"When you like somebody a lot, you like to know things about them."

"Well, I'm *me*! I'm not my parents!" he barked fiercely.

I couldn't keep my face from showing how wounded I was.

"Ginny," he said, softening, "my parents just get me upset."

He took my hand. I hung back. He pulled me close to him. I could see the sadness in his eyes. I stopped resisting.

The kiss went on for a long time, a kiss like sailing off the edge of the world, a kiss that seemed to be all I had ever wanted.

When we moved our lips apart, Hal's eyes betrayed a flicker of surprise, and his face seemed unguarded, defenseless, and then he sprang into action, probably to cover up what he was feeling, grabbing my hand and running with me toward a mound of fallen leaves, and the two of us flung ourselves into the crisp, bouncy mass of autumn colors.

The reason I pondered over that kiss the next day and the day after that and for many days more was that Hal, once again, just like after our sailboat date, didn't telephone me, and when I saw him in school, he didn't ask me out for the coming weekend. And I began worrying about what might have turned him off. This is crazy, Ginny, I warned myself. You had that wonderful time in the sailboat, and he didn't call because he wasn't sure you had a good time. Now you had a wonderful time in Webster Park, and a kiss that girls dream about, and again he doesn't call? Did he think you were putting on an act? How blind can he be?

I also thought, why don't I call him? But suppose I called and suppose he said no? Forget it.

Friday came and then Saturday, and I turned down three different boys who asked for dates, just so I could be available in case Hal asked me. But he didn't call.

My thoughts kept turning to Rita, since she had arranged the movie date that previously broke the ice between Hal and me.

Finally, on Monday afternoon I couldn't stand it any more. I dialed Rita's number, planning to hang up if Hal answered. I listened and listened to the ring and pause, ring and pause. Then I heard Rita answer.

"Rita, can I talk to you? I'm so confused."

"Come on over!"

"Is Hal there?"

"He won't be home for hours."

When I arrived and saw the welcome in Rita's face, I knew I could tell her anything.

"How's your painting?"

"Hard, but good."

"You've been busy."

"You, too. Ginny, I hope you didn't mind what I did that night, the movie, you and Hal?"

"I'm grateful. Rita, I don't know what's happening with Hal and me."

"Hal needs you, Ginny."

"Rita, tell me, please, is he dating other girls?"

"No, he isn't."

That's when I started explaining to her how I felt about Hal. We talked a long time.

"I don't know about your part in it, but I can tell you what's bothering Hal."

"Please, Rita."

She hesitated a moment. Rubbing her palm along the wheel of her chair, she said, "It's about our parents.

"You see, Ginny, my parents—we love them so much—" Her voice choked up for a moment, she bit her lip, trembling, and tears suddenly spilled over her eyelashes, and she buried her face in her hands, sitting there in the wheelchair with her shoulders bent, her body wracked with sobs.

I put my arm around her.

"Thanks, Ginny. You're a good friend."

"I wish," I said.

"My mom and dad—" she got control of her

voice—"we had such great times, and then Dad lost his job, Mom had to work, Dad got jealous, depressed, and the fights began, terrible, terrible fights. Finally Dad walked out. Mom just fell apart. Then she got this research job, twenty-four hours a day kind of job. It was just what she needed to get her mind straight, but she had to go to Mexico, so Hal and I came to stay with Uncle Jeff. Ginny, I miss them so much!"

I held her, and she cried. She had seemed so strong to me, her eyes laughing and welcoming, bursting with life and ideas, never letting the fact of her wheelchair stop her from reaching out, and now I realized she was also strong enough to reveal her secret anguish to me.

"And Hal became so bitter," she said, when she had found her voice again, "he won't even try to understand Mom and Dad, but it's eating at him all the time. So he started throwing himself into all this hang gliding and scuba diving and whatnot, as if he *wants* to get hurt. That's why I was so happy he found *you*."

I kissed her on the forehead. "Thanks, Rita."

"How about a hot chocolate?" she asked, laughing in a sweet, almost shy, kind of way and wiping the tears from her face with the palms of her hands.

I didn't stay with Rita much longer, for fear of running into Hal. We kissed each other goodbye, and I walked away from her house. I walked until my feet were sore. I needed time to absorb what she had told me. Hal must be so torn up about his parents.

Of *course* he must be afraid of falling in love. Of *course* he misjudges how I feel about him. If both my parents suddenly walked out on me, I'd be suspicious, too. No wonder he doesn't want people to see he cares for me; if I do to him what his parents did, at least no one but Rita would know.

I wanted to help him. I wanted to *reach* him, the him that figured the world was a mess.

An idea. Sort of a new strategy. A new recipe for a soup called Cream of Hal and Ginny. Maybe, maybe, maybe what he needed from me, what would help him open up, help him get outside his bad feelings about his parents and help him get interested in sharing my interests and in us getting to really know each other, would be for me to prove I cared enough about him to share all the wild, risky things he was into.

It might work.

Are you ready, Ginny? Are you ready for hang gliding in a Dacron kite a thousand feet up and a crosswind flips you over? Or scuba diving, your oxygen tank fails, a barracuda sidles up and desires your toenails for brunch? And how about, maybe for starters, asking Hal to let his boa constrictor take a stroll around your elbow?

Chapter Fourteen

Except for the evergreens and the oaks with their stiff copper leaves still clinging, all the trees were slowly stripped bare during the next few weeks of windy mornings and nights. Meanwhile, my recipe for Cream of Hal and Ginny boiled and bubbled.

Step one was to get invited to dinner. That was easy. I phoned Rita and asked if she still needed help redecorating Hal's room.

"Believe it or not, the room is *finished.* Ginny, I'm so proud of it! Will you come to dinner so that we can show it off?"

Step two would be—as I stood in the spruced-up room with Rita and (hopefully) Hal—to ask him casually, very casually, as if it was the insignificant whim of a moment, if I might hold his boa constrictor.

I figured if I had the willpower to handle a snake, I might actually be insane enough to strap myself into a scuba tank or a hang glider.

So, for five days before the dinner date, morning till night, I gave myself all kinds of positive suggestions about Hal's boa constrictor: "You are calm. You are brave. You love animals. The snake is an animal. Therefore, you love the snake. The snake will feel your love. The snake will recognize you as a friend. You are calm. You are brave. You—"

A boa constrictor when he gets hungry, according to *Snakes For Everybody*, doesn't dream of vanilla fudge ice cream with marshmallow topping and walnuts. No, his taste buds, if he has any, long for what the book called "warm-blooded prey." Mmm-hm. Boas have needle-sharp teeth capable of severe bites. Owing to the foulness of the snake's mouth, these little love bites can actually lead to blood poisoning. Ugh! Infinity ugh!

To put it mildly, my heart was in my mouth.

Cooking the dinner with Rita, beef roulade, was fun. It was amazing the way she managed in her wheelchair. Setting the table with Rita and Hal was fun, although he seemed— not distant, exactly—a little removed. And eating the dinner with Rita and Hal and their uncle, who kept twitching his screwy little black mustache and telling anecdotes about the construction business, was fun.

The only nonfun was when Uncle Jeff asked if Hal had read the letter from his dad. Hal clenched his teeth and jabbed his fork into his steak.

When dinner was over, I said, "I'm dying to see how you decorated the room."

"Hal did all the really hard work."

"The ideas were yours, Rita."

"Ginny thought of the rainbow, didn't you, Ginny?"

When I entered it, Hal's room made me yelp with delight: there were rich ocean colors on three walls and a brilliant rainbow curving across the fourth, and a new ultramarine carpet. The desk and bureau and bookcase were painted deep blue with small white clouds.

"And I love the way you did the cage!"

"That was your idea, too!"

The glass and wire cage, surrounded by potted plants and floor lights in a corner of the room, gave the impression of a small jungle. The boa constrictor lay like a coiled whip, absolutely motionless among the wood shavings and chips.

Maybe it's dead, I hoped. Can snakes get hardening of the arteries? The creature began to slide forward in my direction. Now or never, Ginny!

"Say, Hal,"—I nearly choked on the words— "could I hold your snake?"

Hal's eyes snapped open in surprise, but he was quick to unlatch the cage, scoop up the boa—actually about three feet long but appearing to me about the length of a football field—and before a scream could burst from my mouth to shatter my phony expression of casual interest, the thing lay coiled coldly over my arm, its eyes with weird vertical pupils almost hypnotizing me.

To my amazement, it wasn't as horrible as I had thought.

"Does it have a name?" I inquired, acting as nonchalant as you can when your throat feels stuffed with cotton and your lungs have almost gone out of business.

"I call him Julius," Hal said.

I began to quiver as the boa began slithering slowly, icily, across my forearm, its smooth scales saying how-do-you-do to a crowd of goose pimples.

"Julius Squeezer," Hal continued. "I think he likes you."

Then the conversation calmly turned back to the possibility of rearranging Hal's bookshelves and gluing mirror tiles on his closet door.

I felt pretty proud of myself, chatting away with Hal and Rita, as Julius Squeezer made a few trips up and down my arm.

Apparently my performance with Squeezer must have affected Hal, bringing me closer to him in some way, because later on, in his car driving back to my house, he did two unusual things.

One, he expressed a worry. I had never heard him express a worry. "You think Rita seems OK?" he asked.

"Far as I can see, sure."

"She's got herself so wrapped up in her painting, I hardly get a chance to talk to her."

"I guess she loves it, Hal."

"Lately, when I offer to take her places, she just wants to stay glued to her paintbrush and canvas. Tells me not to call her so often to see if she's OK. And she's stubborn. When I call more than once, she won't answer the phone. What do you think, Ginny?"

"She sure seems happier than most of us."

And the other unusual thing Hal did, as he walked me from his car to the door of my house, was to ask my advice.

"Ginny, do you really think I should apply for college?"

At first I thought he was kidding, but his voice and his eyes seemed to indicate that my opinion mattered. A secret pleasure rippled through me.

"Gee, Hal, do you want to go to college?"

"Maybe," he murmured, watching my face.

Our hands came together as we stood at the door. I decided to risk a little more.

"How's your hang gliding?"

"I'm working up to my first launch from a real cliff."

"Must be thrilling."

"Would you like to come hang gliding with me?"

"Are we going to hang together or separately?"

Grinning, he roped his wrists around my waist.

"Do you really want to teach me?"

"You'll love it, Ginny. It's like—like—I don't know. You're up there with nothing but you and the kite and the sky, and—and—I must sound like a half-wit!"

"No, you don't."

His mouth reached for mine. It was a relaxed kiss, a peaceful kiss, a trusting kiss, as if for the first time, we were both letting go.

*   *   *

So it seemed as if my frigid friendship with
Hal's snake had set in motion the kinds of
changes I'd been hoping for.

But handling a hang glider, as I discovered
in the following weeks, was far more frightening than the boa constrictor.

The gusty, chilly autumn weather gave way
to a period of warm sun and steady temper-
ate wind. It was during this warm spell that
Hal began instructing me on how to handle
the kite on the ground, how to balance it,
how to use the harness and the riser straps
connecting the harness to the tubular frame,
how to hook on just before take-off and disconnect immediately upon landing.

"You're ready for your first take-off."

Hal's words made jelly out of my knees.

We drove to the sand dunes, where Hal
chose a particularly high one.

"Wind's about ten miles per hour. Just
right."

Hal carried the nose of the hang glider, and
I carried the tail. We set the folded glider on
the ground with the nose pointed directly
into the wind. We rigged the turnbuckles,
connected the Dacron sails to the aluminum

crossmembers, secured the bottom rigging to the control bar, and tightened all the turnbuckles to the point where the cables had no slack.

"It's all yours, Ginny."

I carried the kite uphill to a point with a twenty-foot vertical drop. I had practiced running with the kite, but my feet had never left the ground. The next step was getting off into the air, ground skimming they call it, at twenty miles per hour.

At the bottom of the hill, Hal was beaming.

Put on helmet, connect harness and self to kite, pick up kite, angle nose of kite upward so Dacron sail is just barely inflated by smooth winds coming in off the water, grip for take-off, shoulders wedged lightly between uprights, point directly into wind, begin run downhill, gain speed, thrust forward, running and balancing at the same time, begin angling nose upward by pushing out on control bar.

The Dacron sail, like a huge yellow wing protecting me from the sun, grabbed the air and lifted me off my feet. It was a sudden freedom, sliding down the wind, the sunlight dazzling on the waves.

"Nose up! Nose up!"

I didn't react fast enough. I hit hard.

"Ginny, are you hurt?"

I coughed out about a quarter-pound of sand.

"No, I enjoy having sand for lunch."

"Your leg is bleeding."

"That leg has always had bad habits."

He smiled appreciatively, untangling me from the harness. "You're terrific, Ginny! And the kite isn't even damaged! I'll get a bandage for your leg."

I watched him sprint through the sand toward his car. He had no idea I was half an inch from bursting into tears and having a tantrum!

A few days later, fortunately for me, the weather did another about-face, back to the gusty cold winds that made more hang gliding impossible.

And with the weather change, I began to look for, hope for, even imagine, more signs of Hal changing.

Yes, he seemed less uptight with me. Yes, he seemed less touchy. Was that because I was sharing his interests, or because I was acting less sensitive and uptight myself?

But the truly *important* things did *not* change. He did not hug me in public; he did not stop hanging around in school with other girls. I longed to talk and talk with him about *us*, but I was afraid he'd hate it.

So I kept on trying to win his trust, rather than demand that he change and maybe lose him.

Would you believe *me* in a black rubber wet suit and black flippers, plodding over the seashells in the ocean at South Beach on Saturday, the twenty-eighth of November at twelve thirty-five in the afternoon?

Rita had loaned me the wet suit she herself was no longer able to use.

"There's a thin layer of water between your skin and the rubber, so your body heat warms the layer of water and keeps you insulated." Hal's explanation sounded very comforting. "Otherwise, your heart would probably stop."

I didn't dare ask him what happens if your wet suit springs a leak.

How I managed to keep up with Hal that afternoon, as we flippered our way around the sandy bottom of the protected cove he had chosen to dive in, I'll never know. The sunlight filtering down through the water cast quivering shadows everywhere, and I was positive that every shadow was a creature of the deep out to try its new false dentures on something soft and tasty like me. A newspaper headline kept writing itself in my mind: Girl Succumbs to Killer Whale, Floating Flippers

ALL THAT REMAIN OF SPARKLING HIGH-SCHOOL SENIOR.

Was the kiss, later, in Hal's car—the heat of the car like heaven after the dark and chill of the sea—worth it? Oh, yes.

I snuggled close to him as he put the car in gear. With my eyes closed, the motion of the car made it feel like the dark, mysterious world below the surface of the sea, full of secrets. Like the secrets we have from other people and even from ourselves, secrets and fantasies. Did Hal have a fantasy world of his own like mine? What were his secrets?

Hal kept his eye on the road, his hands sliding back and forth along the steering wheel. A smell of seaweed from the specimens we had gathered filled the car. We seemed so close, yet maybe each of us had so much concealed that even a lifetime wouldn't be enough to share it.

And maybe I was fooling myself, but I detected all kinds of mysteries in the way Hal tightened his hands on the wheel and the way he narrowed his eyes when he glanced into the rearview mirror.

And I started another movie scene in my imagination: Hal as Gregory Peck and I as Ingrid Bergman, both of us on skis, facing downhill on a dangerous snow-covered mountain.

"It's no use," Hal would say, tight-lipped. "My mind is going, and you know it. I killed once, and I might kill again. I'm a split personality."

"No! I can help you if you let me. You killed no one. It's only a fantasy. The secrets you haven't shared are poisoning your mind."

"And suppose you're wrong? Suppose as we ski close to the edge of that cliff, I suddenly become a criminal personality and push you off?"

"I'll take that risk!" I would answer passionately. "Together we can uncover the hidden things in your mind that are torturing you."

"You're quite a woman. All right, I'll try. What do you want me to do first?"

And I would burst out. "The first thing I want you to do is stop sitting with those other girls in the lunchroom!"

I could say it in my imagination, but I sure couldn't say it for real.

And wouldn't you know it, the very next day in the school lunchroom there he was, a smile on his face like a slice of watermelon, sitting opposite a goofy, pretty girl with a punk-rock hairdo and purple fingernails.

And wouldn't you know it, to add a little whipped cream and chocolate sprinkles to the occasion, Pam waved me over joyously to sit with her and a tall, bony guy with nice blue eyes and long sandy hair pulled back in a ponytail.

"Ginny, this is Dave Dutton. Dave"—her eyelids, thick with mascara, fluttered up and down in a shy, sexy way that I last remembered from her early days with Bert—"this is my best friend, Ginny Barnes."

Pam did most of the talking while I tried courageously to slice and swallow the plastic frankfurters served by the school cafeteria. She and Dave kept peppering each other with adoring, cowlike looks and reaching their fingers out to touch each other slyly, as if to make sure they were real.

"When did *this* happen?" I yearned to blurt out at Pam, but didn't. "You just dropped Bert after all these months when you hardly knew I was alive except to use me as a sounding board for your troubles, and now Bert is gone, and suddenly you're cuckoo about another one?"

Dave had to leave lunch early for a squad meeting or something, and the moment he was gone Pam squeezed my arm, moaning ecstatically. "He's crazy about me, Ginny! It's wild! And he's so *honest*. He even admits he doesn't like my nose!"

As she rattled on, listing the virtues of being mad about Dave Dutton, I caught a glimpse of Hal and his punk-rock girl leaning across the lunch table toward each other, heads almost touching, and I hated him more than I'd ever hated anyone; I hated so much it hurt, because I guess I realized I loved him.

Chapter Fifteen

The headlights of Hal's car splashed across scrub grass and sandy waste and here and there a dune laced with wild roses as we bumped along a dirt road and came to a halt facing the beach. We sat arm in arm, my cheek against his shoulder, watching as the foam-tipped waves, caught in the beams of the headlights, tumbled one on top of another. Hal switched off the lights. Through the windshield the freezing black sky filled with stars.

"Want to hear the radio?"

"Let's sit like this a minute more."

The warmth and silence and darkness made the car the cockpit of a spaceship traveling through the universe toward some unknown destination.

"The stars."

"Yeah."

His fingertips pressed against the bones in my shoulder. I knew he wanted to hear the radio, so I pushed the button. Sounds of merrymakers and cheering and blowing horns sprang out at us, and then voices singing "Auld Lang Syne."

"Happy New Year, Ginny," he said softly.

"Happy New Year, Hal."

"Are you sorry we didn't go to a party?"

"Not really."

Our lips touched and parted and touched again and parted, and when they touched for the third time, it was like our mouths had wills of their own, two individual mouths joining to become one. The kiss seemed to last forever, and I was dying to cry out, "I love you, Hal! I love you! I'll always love you!"

Would I ever dare to tell him?

And was it possible that he loved me back?

If he loved me, would he allow the presence of other people to inhibit him from kissing me or holding my hand?

If he loved me, would he allow me to sit with other boys in the lunchroom while other girls made eyes at him?

If he loved me, would it even matter that

he was troubled about his parents splitting up?

If he loved me . . .

Did I have any right to ask him to change? Oh, sure, I had bruises and black-and-blue marks and sore muscles from the hang gliding and the skin diving, but did that really give me any right?

About a week after New Year's Eve, I had a talk with my sister Laura concerning Hal. It really set a time bomb ticking.

"Ginny? Mind if I come in?" Laura asked through the closed door of my room after knocking several times with no response from me.

"OK," I said halfheartedly.

Laura entered with that look I knew so well from all the times before in our lives when she had decided to play Florence Nightingale with me.

"Mind if I sit down on the bed?"

I shook my head. I felt exhausted. It was Sunday afternoon. I'd been lying in bed since I had wakened. No appetite. Smiling weakly when Mom and Dad had come in to ask if I was sick. Not sick. Not physically sick. I couldn't tell them I was bothered about Hal, because it seemed as if I was making a big deal over nothing. Any other girl would be delighted to have a nice boyfriend like Hal and not get so tortured over the way he spent some of his lunch hours.

"How's Alan?" I asked disinterestedly.

A shadow passed across her face. "Working, as usual."

"He works hard."

She brushed her fingertips across her forehead as if she were cleaning away some cobwebs. "Too hard," she said.

"I guess it's better than a husband who's too lazy to earn a living."

Laura took my hand. "We're having problems, Ginny. I started seeing a marriage counselor."

"Alan, too?"

"Not yet. He says he's happy I'm getting help, but he doesn't feel he needs counseling. I guess he thinks I should get my act together and not be so bothered that he works eight days a week."

"Do you agree with him, Laura?"

"I think if we're going to make it, we both have to work on it together."

"I guess men aren't as interested in changing, are they, Laura?"

"Seems that way."

"Yeah."

"Ginny, I didn't come in here to get you depressed about Alan and me. You're having your own problems."

"Who told you?" I jerked my hand away resentfully. I didn't like people talking about me and my problems.

"Everybody who loves you can feel it. Mom and Dad sense you want to work it out by yourself. Do you?"

"Yes, Laura, I do," I replied aggressively.

"Oh," she said, injured by my tone of voice. She stood up, squared her shoulders, then rubbed her lip wistfully.

"I'm finding out," she said almost apologetically, "that I don't have the guts to demand what I need. I hope *you* do, Ginny."

Laura left. I sat staring at a photograph of Hal, water and sunlight glistening on his body as he stood on a surfboard speeding down the avalanching curve of a huge wave.

Is that my problem? I said to myself. I don't have the guts?

The first snowfall of the winter came tumbling down in big wet flakes that melted on my coat as I waited for the bus to school. It was the Monday after I saw Laura. Her words kept haunting me, even when I dashed up the steps into school and, later, moved mechanically from class to class. "I don't have the guts to demand what I need," echoed back and forth inside my head.

And then during lunch hour, Hal wasn't there with another girl, he wasn't there at all, but Pam sure was, holding hands with her beloved Dave. And while I was worrying about Hal, Pam announced proudly, "Ginny, you're the first person we're telling. Dave and I are engaged, as of this weekend!"

Her eyes were filled with such pride and pleasure, and (I thought meanly) a sense of triumph, because she was the first girl of all the girls we knew at school to actually become *engaged.*

"Congratulations," I said, in as strong a voice as I could muster, but inside I felt like a weakling, a failure. Here was Pam getting engaged within a few weeks of meeting Dave (I didn't really believe their parents would *allow* it) while I couldn't even get Hal to go steady with me.

I felt like screaming and biting and scratching and kicking and sobbing and having a tantrum, all rolled into one, but I managed instead to arrange my face in an artificial smile and pat Pam's arm and murmur in a syrupy voice, "That is really fabulous news."

Then I mumbled some excuse about home-work and sailed out of the lunchroom as quickly as I could.

Chapter Sixteen

My forefinger gripped the trigger of the nickel-plated .25-caliber pistol, cold and hard as ice. The gun barrel was aimed slightly to the left of Hal's solar plexus.

"I want answers!" I said, scowling and waving the snout of the pistol threateningly under his nose. "Number one, your secret code. Two, the names of all your agents. Three, how you plan to sabotage our peace conference. Four, where your weapons are concealed. Five, your true identity."

The jagged scar on Hal's jawbone twitched as he spoke. "You must believe me. I'm a double agent, actually working for *your* side."

"Prove it!"

The engines of warplanes roared overhead. The whine of bombs penetrated the walls of the dark cellar where I held my gun on him.

"Contact the White House," he said. "Use the code words Black Boa."

Exploding bombs shook plaster and dust from the ceiling. Hal made a sudden move toward me. My finger tightened on the trigger, a shot rang out, he fell, clutching his heart. I held him in my lap as he breathed his last. "The secret code is—" His head fell limp. . . .

The movie in my mind stopped dead.

Back in reality, snowflakes were covering my hair and shoulders. Several blocks away, the roof of Hal's house was wearing a white toupee. I stared at his house. I had been walking alone in the snow, building up the courage to confront him.

But every time I neared his house, I turned away. Was it just fear that he'd reject me if I expressed my true feelings? Or was it guilt, because I didn't want to add to his problems?

Anyway, at the last moment, as I neared the lawn of his house, my feet did a fast about-face, and I took me and my snowflakes back home. I kept telling myself, *of course he's afraid to care for someone after he saw his own parents break up.* That's why he's always starting and stopping, calling, then not calling. That's the reason.

But the reason began to wear thin, awfully thin.

Every time I saw him with some female in the lunchroom or study hall or wherever, I tried to grit my teeth and bite my tongue. But the trouble with stuffing feelings inside you is that sooner or later they get infected like sores, until even the lightest touch is excruciating.

And it didn't help that Pam's big thing with David, engagement no less, had spread all over the school. Eat your heart out, Ginny, it isn't fattening!

Well, the volcano finally erupted, I guess it had to, all that lava bubbling inside me.

My seventeenth birthday triggered it. I had hoped Hal would remember my birthday; months before, I had mentioned to him that George Washington and I were almost born on the same date. I came two days before George.

Hal forgot my birthday. No doubt he had other problems on his mind. For me, however, his forgetting was the straw that broke the camel's back. The camel looked at herself in the mirror of the girls' bathroom, all seventeen years of her, the day after her birthday, and proceeded to march, hoofs beating, into the school lunchroom.

Tidal waves, land mines, and electric carving knives were disco dancing in my tummy as I stalked across the lunchroom toward Hal and a redhead.

"Hello, Hal!" I said loudly, hoping that the whole lunchroom would hear me.

"Ginny!" He jumped up with a look of delight, but I wasn't about to be cooled down by any big welcome.

"Do you know Carolee Huntington?" he went on enthusiastically.

"No, Hal, I do not know Carolee Huntington, and I do not *want* to know Carolee Huntington," I said, biting into the words as the redhead exchanged a worried glance with Hal. "Carolee, if you happen to get a shark bite or a snakebite or a hole in your glider or a falling rock between the eyes, don't worry. Hal will come to your rescue."

Carolee gaped, completely bewildered.

"And as for you, Hal, darling, I want you to know that our relationship has filled my cup to overflowing. As a matter of fact, my cup runneth over!"

With that I picked up Hal's cup of milk

and poured it over his beautiful honey-colored hair.

My last image of him, as I turned and stormed out of the lunchroom, was of the white beads of milk dripping from his thick, arched eyebrows.

Chapter Seventeen

There was no sense of victory in my lunch-room extravaganza with Hal and the redhead; defeat was what gripped me, total defeat, and on the following day I stayed home, aching all over, drained, and bedraggled. I had absolutely no energy, no appetite, and I had a slight temperature. I woke up and slept, woke up and slept.

Dr. Goldman, when he examined me, said I was very rundown and badly needed a rest. I stayed in bed for a week.

"Could it be psychosomatic?"

Dr. Goldman cocked his head to one side and scratched his earlobe. "Possibly." He knew me from my diaper days, and, I sensed, could see right through me.

"Having problems?"

"Working them out."

"Good. You're right about the psychosomatic aspect. A person's mental state can cause quite a variety of symptoms—headaches, ulcers, you name it."

Can you get ulcers in your heart? I didn't ask him.

How I had the nerve to expect that Hal would call me, I don't know. I guess I figured if our relationship meant anything at all to him, he wouldn't let a cup of milk stop him. Or even if he didn't care that much, at least you would think he'd be curious as to why I gave him the milk treatment.

Well, he didn't care, and he wasn't curious, not for the first three days I was sick.

On the fourth day, his voice, when I picked up the ringing phone, sounded shallow.

"I heard you're sick."

"Yep."

"You OK?"

"Nope."

"You see a doctor?"

"Yep."

"Is it serious?"

"Nope."

"Ginny?"

"Yep?"

"Why did you spill milk on my head?"

150

I hung up.

Hal called back. "I want you to tell me what's bothering you."

"Nope."

"Will you stop that yep and nope!"

He was mad, and I was glad.

"You're angry at me," he said.

"When did you get your private detective's license?"

He was silent for a moment. I said grudgingly, "I'm sorry I did that to you."

"I'd like to know what made you so angry," he said impatiently.

"Forget it."

If he didn't realize I needed him to want to go steady with me, I wasn't going to force the idea on him, that was for sure.

"I thought we were having a great time together," he muttered.

"We were."

"What happened?"

"Nothing."

"You don't dump milk on someone for nothing."

"Hal, I said I'm sorry I dumped the milk on your head. Next time I won't dump it on you. I'll dump it on somebody who won't keep bothering me for an explanation."

"Do you realize that now everybody in school

thinks that you and I had some tremendous secret going on?"

"Well, we did."

"What secret? We were dating, that's all."

"OK, Hal. We didn't have any secret. You didn't have any secret. I didn't have any secret. Fine."

"I can't figure you out, Ginny."

"I can't figure you out, either."

"Just like that, no reason, you drop my milk on my head."

"Just like that, Hal."

The silence between us on the phone got bigger and bigger.

"Are we going to keep dating?" he said.

I should have said yes. I should have said yes and then carefully explained exactly how I felt and why I felt what I did.

But I didn't say anything.

"I'll see you around, Ginny. Get well soon."

Chapter Eighteen

I almost wanted to die. I didn't really, but I almost did.

I even imagined me on my deathbed, a shadow of my former self, smiling weakly at poor Hal as he put his head between his hands and sobbed and with my last breath I said to him tenderly, "You tried your best, Hal, but your best just wasn't good enough. . . ."

What was wrong with me that I couldn't be straight-out honest with him, that I had to let things build up to a world war?

While I was resting at home, Pam called every day and wanted to visit me, but I knew she'd just go on yakking about David, and so I begged off seeing her. She also sent me a get-well card with a box of maple sugar hearts.

It *was* sweet of her. Maybe I hadn't paid

enough attention to her lately. Maybe I'd been too wrapped up in myself and my problems with Hal.

School, when I went back, was a drag. I did my work, but without enthusiasm. I avoided Hal. Whenever I saw him, I gave a phony smile and kept going.

As for Pam, as usual her life was a seesaw.

"How's David?" I said to her my first day back in school.

"Fine," she said listlessly. She looked thinner and a little sad.

"Are you planning on a long engagement?"

"I don't know."

"What's the matter, Pam?"

"I should be happy."

"You're not happy?"

"David is so nice. But—I miss Bert. And my father keeps bugging me about my school grades. And you and I don't get any time together. And my mother seems so depressed. And I just hate myself for whining all the time. It's so confusing!"

"I'm sorry, Pam. Listen, I'll talk to you later. I have to see my French teacher."

I knew she wanted a lot of support from me, but I was irritated that she hadn't asked me one question about how I felt and why I had dumped the milk on Hal.

But then it occurred to me that the bad feelings I was having for Pam were a lot like the bad feelings I had for Hal. Neither one of them seemed to care much about *my* true interests, *my* true feelings, *my* problems.

Maybe it wasn't all their fault. Maybe it was something in my personality that made them think I didn't want to talk about me.

Well, my spirits were really pretty low, and they stayed low as the March weather zigzagged back and forth from springlike days to days of scattered snow, rain, cold with skies the color of lead, and a piercing wind.

My mind kept turning to Rita.

How did she keep her spirits up, I began wondering. Wheelchair, parents split up— sure, she had cried, but somehow she seemed to have a strength. I missed her.

So I arranged to see her.

We sat alone in her uncle's backyard. Hal, I knew, was at work. The air was cool, but the sun felt good.

"How do you do it, Rita?"

"What?"

"Be happy."

"It's easy."

"Oh, sure."

"All you have to do is try to stop *expecting*."

"You think I expect a lot?"

"I can only speak for myself. The more I expect people to make me happy, the more I get miserable."

"But your friends are *supposed* to try to make you happy, that's what friends are for."

"After my accident, I was terribly depressed. For months. Sure, people tried to make me happy, but it didn't work. Finally, I found something that worked."

"What did you find?"

"Trying to make other people happy. Forgetting about myself. I just felt good when I could do something for somebody. And very often, when I least expected it, people would make me happy, too. But the only happiness I have any control over is the happiness of trying to make someone else happy. That—and painting, creating—works."

What Rita was saying took a long time to sink in. Only days and weeks and months later did I begin to understand.

Chapter Nineteen

Down in the dumps over Hal, yes, but still afraid to take a step in his direction, and I had absolutely no desire to be with other boys.

What cheered me up, unfortunately only temporarily, were the tips of the crocuses pushing up out of the soil around our house where Mom had planted them. In a few swampy places along the road I had seen the purple tips of the skunk cabbages, which meant spring, and spring made me think maybe I wouldn't be depressed forever.

Snow fell on the first day of spring—talk about disappointment—and buried all the young new sprouts and buried me along with them. Getting depressed is rotten because it never seems as if you have a good enough reason to be depressed, which makes you feel even more depressed.

What pulled me out of my depression was a phone call from Mrs. Harley. She desperately needed a baby-sitter for the afternoon, the first-day-of-spring afternoon, and I jumped at the chance to get out of my rut.

That's how come Jason and I ran around in the snow in their backyard for hours, near the new addition that Hal's uncle had constructed for Mrs. Harley. My joy at playing with little Jason was tinged with sweet-and-sour memories of those first days when Hal had jumped off the back of the truck and when I had removed his splinter and. . . . Well, Jason and I got good and soaked, went inside to warm up, got happy on ginger ale—I was happy to see he still needed me for a ginger ale fix, I wasn't completely useless—and, after drying off, we ran outside again to build a snow fort and blast each other with snowballs. In the middle of our battle, Jason stopped suddenly and gave me the saddest, queerest, most puzzled look.

"What's coming out of your eyes?" he asked.

"It's uh. . . ." I turned my head away.

"And down your cheeks," he said, peering at me intently.

I was crying—don't ask me why—and thinking of the good times with Hal and feeling weirdly beautiful inside for no reason.

That's when, out of the blue, I felt a rush of appreciation for what Rita had told me about happiness and expectations and love.

And I raced home, after Mrs. Harley had returned, swept up with excitement about calling Hal, a flood of hope that maybe I could learn to love somebody as much as I was able, without always measuring how much I got back against how much I gave, just trying to learn how to give and enjoy the giving.

Up the stairs and into my room I ran, ready to stretch out on my bed with the phone to call Hal.

On my bed was a sealed envelope. Sometimes Mom put the mail on my bed if she thought it was really important. The letter was from Rita.

Dear Ginny,

You are the best thing that happened to us since we moved here. I say us because I know that Hal feels the same way. I know you needed time to think and be with yourself; that's the only reason I haven't called you, didn't want to intrude. But now, unfortunately, I have to tell you goodbye. Perhaps I should have called you, but I'm feeling so excited, terrified, happy, that I didn't trust myself to talk over the phone without blubbering all over the receiver. So I'm writing instead to tell you that my mom and dad have decided to try again as a family and have sent us plane tickets to join them in San Diego. I will always remember you and be grateful.

Love,
Rita

P.S. Our plane leaves on Saturday.

Chapter Twenty

"What about graduation?"

"I'll graduate at my old school in San Diego."

"Did you have a lot of friends there?"

"Some."

"So many people get divorced, I'm glad at least your parents are making another try."

Hal's jaw tightened as he tried to respond with a grin, but the grin was halfhearted. "Yeah, people are getting divorced so fast these days, they even fight over custody of the wedding cake."

Seeing him try so hard to be cheerful, I almost wanted to cry, but I held it in and said instead, "If I ever get married, I'm going to save money and have a wedding pretzel."

"That's not funny, Ginny."

"Neither was yours."

He grinned slyly. "Well, at least we try."

We were sitting on the hull of his Uncle Jeff's sailboat, which was propped up on blocks of wood near the edge of the pier. I had called Hal the moment I read Rita's letter. He had picked me up at my house and then driven us to the boat yard. The boat yard seemed the right place to be.

"I'll miss you," I whispered.

"Me, too."

"I'm sorry I messed things up."

"Ginny, I had the best times of my life with you."

A lump in my throat made it hard to speak. "Really, Hal?"

"The best."

I longed for him to reach out and take my hand, touch my face, hold me. Then I thought, where are your guts, Ginny? Even if it's best to try to love without expecting to get paid back for every nice thing you do, you can still *ask* for things. Just don't get hateful if you don't get what you ask for.

So I asked.

"Will you kiss me, Hal?"

That was the first kiss I ever asked for. I was shaking like a leaf.

He held my face between his hands. He stroked my hair. With the tips of his fingers

162

he traced a pattern on my forehead and my cheekbones. His mouth fitted softly over mine.

A white-hot fountain of sparks flew and fell from the welder's torch in the workshop where a masked mechanic was repairing the steel hull of a sailboat.

"Someday I'll have a forty footer like that one," Hal murmured, both of us catching our breath from the kiss and caught by the spectacle of the fiery sparks plunging from the welder's torch.

"Oh, no!" I almost cried out. "How can you talk about boats when you just kissed me?"

But I stopped myself in time. "Ginny, Ginny, Ginny," I could imagine Rita saying patiently, "stop *expecting* so much from people. Just make sure *you* give as much as you can enjoy giving, and then a little more."

And then I realized that it wasn't only Rita who had taught me that; I had heard it for years from my mom and dad, in one way or another. It was the kind of good advice that you never take to heart until you're desperate.

The wind was picking up. We jumped down from the hull, and Hal slipped his arm around my waist. We walked along the creaky wooden pier, sailboats and motorboats and launches rocking in the last winds of March.

"I hope you get your boat someday," I murmured.

Hal stopped and looked into my eyes as if he were trying to probe every nook and cranny of my being. "A boat," he said, "isn't as important as people."

The thought of him going away from me, maybe forever, the thought I had been pushing and pushing away, fell between us like a wall of glass, and I couldn't endure the pressure of his eyes.

"I wish we were meeting for the first time," he said.

"Why, Hal?"

"I would have done things differently."

"I don't understand."

"A hundred times I wanted to ask you to go steady with me."

"That's crazy!"

A hurt look cramped his face. "Why is it crazy?"

"Because that's what I wanted more than anything!"

"No!"

"Yes!"

"But I saw you so many times with other guys, Ginny."

"Because I saw you with girls."

"But I'd always wave for you to come over!"

"So would I!"

He shook his head. "You seemed so popular, I never thought you'd want to go steady."

"That's what I thought about *you*! That's why I poured milk on you that day."

Tears had sprung to my eyes, and Hal's brow knotted up. He rubbed his forehead with his knuckles. I slipped my hands in the pockets of his jacket, and he held me close, staring across the wind-whipped marina. The muscle in his jaw tightened and relaxed. He wiped away a tear from beneath my eye.

"People keep too many things secret," he said huskily.

"I wanted to tell you—" A huge lump formed in my throat. "I've never told anybody, Hal. People think I'm attractive and intelligent, but they don't know how lonely I sometimes feel. And I can't tell my family how awful I feel because they want me to think I'm wonderful, and if I don't feel I'm wonderful, they think they've failed or something. Sometimes I hate them for expecting so much of me."

Tears flowed freely down my cheeks. "That's my secret, Hal. But I love them, too. You know?"

I turned away from him, ashamed, slapped my forearms down on the wooden railing facing the water, and jammed my chin between my wrists.

Hal leaned over and kissed my forehead.

"I guess I should throw something in the pot, too. My secret, my secret is"—he hesitated, his jaw trembled and tightened, he licked his lips—"sometimes I feel I'm going to have to be responsible for Rita for the rest of my life. Ginny, I can't stand myself for feeling that way, but I don't trust my parents to be around when she needs someone, and there's no one else but me, and sometimes even though Rita is so terrific, I don't want to feel responsible!"

Was that a tear forming in the center of his eye? If so, he brushed it away so quickly with the back of his hand that I couldn't be sure.

We held on to each other in silence. A horn hooted over the water. A two-masted yacht, sails furled, glided slowly toward the marina, its motor hardly audible.

"What do we do now?" he asked.

Chapter Twenty-One

Why is it that, even when they are crowded, airports seem so empty?

Hal hoisted his suitcase and Rita's onto the scale at the airline desk, then turned to me. "Let's take a walk."

He led me away from Rita and their uncle, out the glass doors that swung open as if by magic.

In the open air the sound of a departing jet cut through the sky. Sunlight gleamed on the nose of the huge silvery plane as it angled upward over the airport.

Hal and I walked hand in hand along the concourse that led toward a bronze fountain sculpture of raised eagle wings twenty feet high. Water spouted upward in a tall white bubbling stream.

"I keep thinking we should say something important," he said.

Somehow, spontaneously, I had the courage to answer, "How about 'I love you'?"

"Suppose we don't ever see each other again?"

"Don't say that."

"It could happen."

"I don't care. I love you, Hal."

We walked awhile, past the fountain and, in a circle, back toward the air terminal. He seemed trapped inside himself. I held tight to his arm, trusting.

"I love you, Hal," I said again.

He didn't answer. Strangely, it didn't matter.

But when the glass doors opened for us to enter, he suddenly said, his face sober, "Why do bees hum?"

"Tell me."

"Because they can't remember the words."

Kissing Rita, kissing Hal, watching him push her in her wheelchair toward the gateway and then out of sight, and watching, with their uncle, as their plane lifted off into a pure, blue cloudless sky and headed west . . . I ached. There went two people I loved so much and might never see again. It hurt and hurt, and yet I felt, at the bottom of that hurt, at peace with myself.

And a little while later, when we were in Jeff's car, I even laughed out loud.

"What's so funny?" Jeff twitched his little black mustache.

I had forgotten to ask Hal what the inscription on his ring meant. And also I still didn't know whether he had ever had a steady girl in California.

"I'm just laughing at my mind."

"Your *mind*?"

Uncle Jeff was whistling contentedly, telephone poles and houses moving past our car windows. And I started imagining.

The jungle, a field hospital near the battlefront, shells exploding, Hal stumbles into my arms near the operating room, his blood streaming down my nurse's uniform.

"Hal, you're hurt!"

"I had to come back. Ginny, I . . ."

That's when I decided to stop the movie. I began to think maybe the movies I played in my head were cop-outs.

"What worked for me," Rita had said, "was trying to make other people happy, and not expecting . . ."

I thought of someone who needed me. Someone who needed a friend like Rita. Yes, there was a person definitely needing the kind of friend who cares without expecting anything back and yet also talks through her real feelings now and then.

Pam, I said in my mind, watching the road rush up toward the speeding car and listening to Hal's uncle whistle. I could be that way for Pam.

Pam, and probably lots of other girls and guys.

It could be a real adventure.